Instinctive Heroes

By Sydney Carr

Copyright

Copyright c 2014 Sydney Carr

The moral right of the author has been asserted

All rights reserved. No part of this publication may be produced, stored in a retrieval system or transmitted in any form or by any means without prior permission in writing of the author.

Author's Notes.

This book is the sequel to 'Heroes?' which was also written by Sydney Carr. Although it is not essential that 'Heroes?' is read first, readers may find that by doing so they would add to their enjoyment of this book.

The terrace of the Sixth Row where much of the action in this book takes place is fictional. Whilst the Sixth Row was very much a real place, numbers 50 to 60 depicted within these pages never existed. There were only ever two terraces of the Sixth Row, the fictional short Row in this book would have been located on a small area of allotments sandwiched between the end of the actual Sixth Row and the north end of Cross Row. Hotspur House in High Market depicted in this book is also fictional. All other locations in the book I have described as I remember them in 1958 Ashington.

I have changed the names of two family owned shops that may be familiar to some readers.
All characters in the book are fictional.

Dialogue where appropriate is written in Geordie/Pitmatic dialect with the words spelt phonetically; these are not spelling mistakes or typing errors. For those readers not familiar with this dialect, I have listed the Geordie/Pitmatic words I have used along with their meanings at end of the book. I have not included words that should be easily understood. The pronunciation of Geordie/Pitmatic words I leave entirely to the reader.

Table of Contents

Chapter 1 — Brothers Apart

Chapter 2 — A Returning Threat

Chapter Three — Mary

Chapter 4 — A First Warning

Chapter Five — Frightening Storm

Chapter Six — Homecoming

Chapter Seven — Good Riddance

Chapter Eight — An Explosive Day

Chapter Nine — Recovery

Chapter Ten — Moving On

Chapter Eleven — A Picnic to Remember

Epilogue

Acknowledgement

Geordie/Pitmatic words used in this book

Chapter 1
Brothers Apart

'Bloody shite! Bloody frigging, bloody shite! That's buggared it noo,' fourteen year old Jake Grundy moaned as he surveyed the charred, smouldering outline of the 'Hacky Dorty's' tent that he had been sleeping in just a few minutes earlier. Wearing only his grubby khaki shorts, he wiped a sooty hand across his sweating and blackened face, looked at the primus stove sitting burning innocently where the tent had been and groaned, 'Wait ontil they see this, they'll frigging massacree me!'

An hour earlier, as the hot morning sun had begun to burn through the skin of their tent pitched in the sand dunes between Bamburgh and Seahouses, the rest of the Hacky Dortys; Ian, Rafe, Howard and Reg, had noisily climbed out of their sleeping bags, dressed and had rudimentary ablutions before taking the primus stove out of the ridge tent to boil water for a pot of morning tea. Jake had ignored the jibes, taunts, pushes and kicks his pals had used to try and coax him from under his threadbare blanket. Instead he had wrapped it tighter around himself and rolled up foetus like, refusing to budge.

Tea drunk, the lads had draped their sleeping bags over the spikey coarse grass of the sand dunes to air, put the primus and kettle back inside the tent and after a few more digs at Jake, who responded by farting loudly, they climbed on their bikes in great spirits and headed for the fishing and tourist village of Seahouses.

The heat from the late August sun of 1958 allied with hunger and thirst had finally defeated Jake's attempt to sleep. Throwing his blanket on top of the other lad's neatly stacked packs, he gave his dangly bits a good scratching, pulled on his tatty shorts and took a drink of luke warm water from his ex-army water bottle. Despite having been warned several times by the others not to use the primus stove inside the tent, he filled up the kettle and placed it next to the primus which he turned on and still being full of pressure, it sprayed fuel over the side of the tent! Quickly turning it off, he searched for matches inside the cardboard box containing their meagre supply of food and cooking utensils.

Matches in hand, he knelt in front of the stove and carefully turned it on a fraction and lit a match, touching the flame to the dribble of fuel spluttering from the burner. The result was spectacular – the fuel ignited with a whoosh, the flames leaping up the fuel spattered, sun-warmed sloping roof of the tent that burst into flames, spreading with lightning speed. Minus his eyebrows and most of his eye lashes, a singed Jake began throwing the packs out of the tent but had to quickly abandon the task. The intense heat drove him out of the tent that was being rapidly devoured by the fire, eventually leaving only the two smouldering two uprights and cross poles that were held in place by guy-ropes. Amazed at the speed that the fire had devoured the tent canvas, Jake realised it was the speed that it had burned that had prevented the lad's packs and other bits and pieces inside the tent from being destroyed by the flames.

'Bugga it,' he said aloud, 'Aah need a cup of tea,' and placing the aluminium kettle on the still burning stove, he grabbed a battered box of cornflakes and sat down on a pack to eat the cereal like a bag of crisps as the rising sun burnt his bare, thin shoulders.

Half way round the world, another Grundy had lain uncomfortably in an ambush, sweating and itching and feeling incredibly tense for almost twenty-four long hours. He had just begun to relax as he lay watching the late afternoon sun cast shafts of bright light that penetrated the dense jungle canopy way above his head. But now, lying on the stinking, fetid floor of the Malaysian Jungle, Jake's nineteen-year old brother Ronnie lifted the butt of the light machine gun (LMG) into his shoulder and watched nervously as the voices they had heard a few seconds earlier, drew closer. Next to him Lance Corporal Fred Keating, a garrulous and wiry lad from the Ninth Row in Ashington, held his hand up a few inches indicating 'wait' as the voices on the indistinct footpath to their front morphed into the shapes of eight of the illusive remnants of the Malayan National Liberation Army (MNLA).

Second Platoon of C Company, The Kings Own Northumbrian Border Regiment (KONBR) had deployed into their ambush position twenty four hours earlier, one of six ambush positions hastily deployed in order to capture or kill the last of the communist terrorists fleeing north to Thailand after the surrender of the majority of the terrorists at Telok Anson Marsh, north east of Kuala Lumpur. During the past eighteen months, they had spent numerous fruitless nights and days lying in silent, uncomfortable and mind-numbing ambushes, waiting for an elusive enemy that had never materialised – until today.

Ronnie, Fred and Harry Morris the machine gun loader, watched silently, almost afraid to breathe as the terrorists walked past their cut of position and into the killing zone of the main ambush party a few yards further along the track.

Tired and weary from their forced march through the jungle and believing they were far from any pursuing troops, the terrorists were not fully alert. All of them carried their weapons slung over their shoulders; two were even smoking as they entered the part of the path designated 'The Killing Zone' by the platoon commander, Lieutenant Sebastian Stanley. All but two of them died in ten ear-splitting seconds when the two 'Northumbrian' sections opened up just a tad too early with their two LMGs and sixteen of the new 7.62 self-loading rifles (SLR).

Ronnie had kept the sights of his LMG on the terrorists as they moved out of his view into the killing zone and continued to hold it steady, waiting! Although expected, the sudden deafening cacophony of machine gun and rifle fire startled him but he held his aim even when the two remaining terrorists came sprinting back along the track with their Chinese Type 50 sub machine guns at the ready.

'Halt' shouted Fred but the terrorists kept coming, both firing long bursts at where the shout had come from, forcing Fred and Harry to duck as Ronnie remained calm and squeezed the trigger firing four, five round bursts knocking the fleeing bandits off their feet, killing them instantly.

'Did ye get them Marra,' Fred whispered as the jungle fell silent. The shooting which had lifted hundreds of birds noisily from their perches, had also silenced a troop of gibbons who had been whooping for hours much to the annoyance of the men lying silently in the ambush.

'Aye, Aah got them, tha deed Aah reckon,' Ronnie replied as he breathed again.

After several minutes off silence, the jungle noises began to return and Lieutenant Stanley rose cautiously to one knee and ordered, 'Two Section turnabout and cover rear; One Section advance.'

While his Platoon quickly and efficiently secured the area, removed weapons from the dead terrorists and searched the blood spattered bodies for intelligence, Stanley radioed a 'Contact Report' back to Company HQ, three miles away in an abandoned Kampong.

Six foot two, powerfully built, thirty-five year-old Company Sergeant Major (CSM) 'Big Bill' Armstrong allowed a smile to lighten his stern countenance for the briefest of moments as he listened to Lieutenant Stanley's report crackling through the headset of the Company Radio that the Company Commander (OC), Major Neville Wright held between them. Events then moved quickly, after informing Battalion HQ of the successful ambush, the OC ordered the rest of his Company to move to support Second Platoon and hold the area until the bodies of the terrorists were moved to a helicopter landing site.

Back at the ambush site, Lt Stanley compared each corpse with a photo card of the terrorist hierarchy before walking over to Where Ronnie, Fred and Harry now lay facing outwards behind their LMG, 'Good shooting Grundy, I believe you have just killed Lee Tan, the leader of the terrorists that had refused to surrender but that will have to be confirmed.'

Ronnie asked, 'Did we get them all Sir?'

'Yes all dead and there is a sizeable reward on the head of one the two you killed.'

Two hours later as the rest of the Company relieved a weary but exultant Second Platoon, Big Bill Armstrong stopped Ronnie and Fred as they joined the rest of their Platoon for the two mile walk to the nearest vehicle track. Looking down at the bedraggled, boyishly good looking Ronnie sweating in his olive green uniform and cradling his LMG wearily in his arms, the CSM growled, 'Not bad shooting for a raggy arsed little Ashington git Grundy!'

Ronnie drew himself up to his full five foot eight and replied cheekily, 'Almost as good as a blidy big Newbiggin Giant aye Sir?'

'Watch it Grundy, don't push yer luck son,' Big Bill snapped back.

'Hoo much is the reward for killing that Tan bloke Sir?'

'A few thousand dollars lad but you won't see any of it, we're soldiers not bloody mercenaries; the money goes to the army not little gob-shites like you.'

Ronnie grinned up at the CSM and said 'Thanks very much Sir, so does that mean I get nowt?'

'Exactly lad, but and I mean but, it might help you get the stripe back that we took off you for marrying your little Chinese Madam, now get on with the pair of you.

Back at the beach, torn between buggaring off home or riding after the Hacky Dortys and facing their wrath for destroying the tent they had hired, Jake decided upon the later but not until he had something more to eat.

Searching through the charred cardboard box he was disappointed to find only a packet of 'Smash' potato powder and cursed, 'Sod it,' as the sound of a motorbike came from the other side of the sand dune that hid their wild campsite from the main road.

Mike Trevelyan - formerly Shepherd, switched of the motor of his James Cadet motorbike and flipping out the stand propped it carefully before removing his Helmet and gloves. Unfastening the straps of the rear panniers, he carefully took out several neatly wrapped packages and a couple of biscuit tins. He had enjoyed the ride over from Ashington and looked forward to spending the day with his younger brother Ian and his pals or 'The Hacky Dortys' as they called themselves. Together with the other boy's parents, his mother Jane had prepared food parcels ('Red Cross Parcels' she had called them) and along with a couple of bottles of Dandelion and Burdock, had given them to Mike to deliver to the ever hungry boys.

When he left 'Hotspur House' their new four-bedroomed Edwardian home in High Market, an area of shops built to support the first colliery houses built in the late 19th Century when Ashington was just developing; Jane had walked off with Tommy, her eight-year old son toward Wansbeck Terrace to drop him off at the home of her newly married and very heavily pregnant sixteen-year old daughter Maureen, before walking back to High Market to start her shift at Alice Kirkup's Bakery.

Stacking the parcels carefully, Mike lifted them and walked up and around the sand dune to where he expected to find the tent. He was not expecting the lads to be there and most certainly did not expect to see the sight that greeted him. Jake Grundy's skinny, shorts clad body stood in front of a scene of some devastation while he grinned sheepishly from his soot blackened face!

Of the large ridge tent that had been there, only the poles held in place by guy ropes with burnt shreds of canvas hanging from the cross pole remained, those and the scorched remains that indicated the outline on the ground. Inside these marks were two or three rucksacks, a tatty blanket, a singed cardboard box and a primus stove that was still burning. Outside what had been the tent were another two rucksacks, various water bottles, several sleeping bags spread across the sand dune and, Jake's bike.

Jake dropped the packet of Smash that he had been holding and said to a shocked Mike, 'Hallo Mike got any food?'

Open mouthed and bewildered, Mike stared at the scene for a minute or two before replying, 'Food! Food, niver mind blidy food, what the blidy Hell's happened here and where the Hell are Ian and the rest of them?

'Aah had a bit of an accident that's all man.'

'A bit of an accident, ye've bornt the blidy tent doon man!'

'Am Aalreet like, thanks for asking,' Jake said defensively.

'I can see ye bloody alright but the tent's not noo is it, what happened?'

Mike carefully placed the parcels and tins on the sand as Jake told him of the fire, leaving out the part where the fuel had splashed onto the tent.

'How many times have you been telt ye not te use the burner in the tent man, Aah divvint kna man, yer lucky te be alive.'

'I winnit be for much longa if Aah divvint get sumat te eat soon,' Jake said petulantly while looking hungrily at the parcels Mike had brought.

Mike shook his head and said, 'Right, haway, we'll tidy this lot up then Aah'll ride into Seahooses and tell the lads what has happened; I suppose ye'll all hev te gan hyem tonight seeing as ye hevn't got a tent te sleep in.'

Jake was crestfallen, he had been having a terrific time camping and did not want to go home to the Sixth Row yet, 'We can sleep under tha stars like the cooboys man,' he said hoping Mike would agree.

'Yor nee blidy cowboy Jake, yor a walking blidy disaster man, noo come on and help me sort this lot oot while Aah fetch a couple of bottles of pop up from my bike.'

A few minutes later as Mike rode off toward Seahouses; Jake began to inspect the food parcels and tins!

Mike's Brother Ian, along with their fourteen year old Uncle Rafe and Reg and Howard had spent the morning fishing unsuccessfully from the southern breakwater of the picturesque and bustling harbour at Seahouses. Bored with their lack of success, they stowed their cheap expanding fishing rods into the panniers of their bikes and cycled round the harbour to watch the men working on a new fishing boat outside the boat shed adjacent to the lifeboat station.

A little later, they missed Mike riding slowly down the hill leading to the harbour and around to the far side as they once more climbed onto the bikes and headed back to the tent to see if he had arrived with the latest food parcels from home. They were all hungry and having speculated all morning as to what they would receive, they were looking forward to opening the food parcels when they arrived back at the tent.

Jake had recognised the parcel from his Mam; it was shoddily and unnecessarily wrapped in a copy of The News of the World, unnecessary because it contained an Oxo tin that he knew would be full of sandwiches.

Inside the wrapping was a scribbled note from his Mam saying, *'Jake hav made yor favrit egg and tomata sandwitchis, no fresh tomatas so used tined ones. Tek care Bonny Lad, Mam.'*

Sitting down, he struggled to open the firmly closed lid and held it pressed to his stomach as he finally levered it off, spilling the soggy contents of pulp like, tomato soaked bread and slimy chopped boiled egg onto shorts and bare legs.

Leaping up he brushed the disgusting mess from his shorts and legs and shouted, 'Mam you stupid bugga man, tinned tomatas mek bread gan claggy!'

Undeterred, he opened a very neatly wrapped package that had something solid inside. It was a plate pie and Jake's eyes lit up when he saw it. Aggie Galloway, who lived next door to Mike and Ian's old house in the Sixth Row, had made the corned beef and potato pie along with a mince and onion pie that was in another package. Jake devoured the first pie greedily, washing it down with half a bottle of Dandelion and Burdock before belching loudly and turning to examine the other parcels. Half an hour later lying flat on his back, bloated and feeling just a little nauseas, he heard the voices of his pals approaching!

Having inspected the company's defensive perimeter with Major Wright, Bill Armstrong loosened the buckle of his '1944 pattern' green webbing belt and cradling his sub machine gun, sat down for a smoke break, taking a minute to reflect on the letter he had received from his mother Sarah the night before. The letter had shocked and upset him and he wanted a few minutes to reread it and gather his thoughts on the dreadful news it contained. Taking a plastic pouch from his chest pocket, he opened it and carefully withdrew the flimsy, blue air-mail letter and unfolded it.

His widowed mother still lived in the terraced house that he had been born in North Seaton Road in Newbiggin-by-the-Sea, the house she shared with her widowed sister, Margaret Shepherd. Rubbing the one inch scar above his left eye, Bill re-read the letter slowly; trying to extract every bit of information from his Mother's pithily written news. The dreadful news it contained was that his older cousin and war hero Nick Shepherd had been hanged for the murder of a policeman. Bill found the news difficult to comprehend; he had been in awe of Nick who had won, or so he believed, the Military Medal during the British Expeditionary Forces retreat to Dunkirk. Since joining the army in 1941, Bill had seen very little of Nick who had been invalided out earlier that year due to the wounds he received winning the medal. On the last occasion, the christening of Nick's son Ian, he had watched Nick become a tad drunk and just a little abusive and saw how Jane, Nick's beautiful wife calmed him down, eventually restoring the party atmosphere in their tiny colliery house at the end of the Sixth Row in Ashington.

The letter did not provide much detail on why he had committed murder other than his mother writing that she believed he had been driven to it by a pair of 'Gangsters' named McArdle! She also said that Jane had gone back to using her maiden name – Trevelyan and had moved into a large house in High Market and, that her estranged father had committed suicide, leaving her not only a nice amount of money but also a fourteen year old brother called Rafe who now lived with Jane and her four children. It was a lot to take in and unfortunately his mother had not helped by only providing snippets of information as she endeavoured to keep to the one and a half page 'Bluey.'

'Gangsters in Ashington!' Bill thought, 'if I find they are responsible for Nick's death, they'll bloody well wish they had never been born.'

His thoughts were broken by Major Wright, 'Everything all right CSM, you look as though you've seen a ghost?'

'Everything is fine Sir, just some sad news from home – my cousin has died; we were close once.'

'That is sad news, I'm afraid you will miss his funeral.'

'I've already missed it Sir, he was buried three months ago, my Mam has only just let me know but I will travel to Newbiggin when I fly back to Blighty with the Advance Party next week; there's a couple of things I need to sort out.'

The OC nodded and said, 'Yes this little operation has caused a few problems with our preparations for handing over the Barracks and you handing over the Company to Sergeant Major Shelby. You are lucky to be flying back, I'm not relishing the several weeks we will have to spend on that damn Troop Ship when the Battalion sails in four weeks.'

As darkness swiftly fell, almost as though a switch had been thrown, Two Platoon took nearly three hours of slow hiking along a well-defined path through relatively open jungle to reach the track where they were to meet up with trucks that were to transport them back to a temporary camp on jungle airstrip north of Kuala Lumpur.

Nicknamed 'Olly' the Platoon Sergeant, Jim Cromwell, a tall, wiry and swarthy-skinned man from Alnwick, allocated areas for the three sections to rest and eat, before ordering the section commanders to do another ammunition count.

Ronnie, Fred and Harry dropped their small packs and webbing and using torches, searched their packs for food.

'Aah've got a tin of Mutton Scotch style,' Fred groaned.

'Me too,' said Harry.

'Whey Aah've got a tin of stewed steak and a packet of Chinese spices from Mary.'

Fred looked at his tin of mutton and muttered, 'Frigging shite this man, Aah'll be glad when we get back doon to Singa's and get some proper grub.'

Looking covetously at Ronnie's spices, Harry asked, 'Canna hev sum of your Missus's spices Ronnie?'

'Aye of course ye can,' he replied, 'but am keeping the stewed steak.'

Harry, the youngest of the three by almost two years, was a gregarious, tousled haired lad from Amble who had only joined the Battalion two months previously and was in awe of the other two, especially Ronnie. He looked up to Ronnie whose dark good looks, flashing smile and ready wit, combined with an inner strength and determination that he admired so much. He had seen how determined Ronnie could be when he had defied regulations and married the beautiful Mary Peng and lost his stripe for having done so.

Sprinkling the spices that Ronnie had handed him onto his broth, Harry asked innocently, 'Is yor lass really a prossie then Ronnie?'

Ronnie's face reddened and he scrambled to his feet to attack Harry but Fred leapt in between them holding Ronnie tightly, 'Calm doon Ronnie, the stupid sod doesn't kna his bloody arse from his elbow man!'

Controlling his anger, Ronnie snarled at Harry, 'My wife is not or niver has been a prossie, she ran the Lion Bar with her brother after her mother died, it's the other four lasses there that are prossies and if Aah was ye, I'd be very careful aboot what shite Aah said!'

Looking up sheepishly at Ronnie, Harry almost whispered, 'Am sorry Ronnie marra, Aah didn't mean nowt, Aah must hev hurd wrang like.'

Fred now turned on Harry and snarled, 'Fuck sake man shut yer fucking gob before any more shite comes oot of it or Aah'll give ye a daading!'

Looking down at his food and wishing he wasn't there, Harry muttered, sorry Fred.'

'It's Corporal to you, you fucking retard, you haven't urned the right te call me Fred yet, noo shut the fuck up!'

Seeing how worried the younger lad was, Ronnie nudged his leg with his jungle boot and said, 'Look forget it man, just think before ye speak, and ye are one of us, ye did alright back at the ambush, didn't he Fred?'

'Oh aye, he changed the mag on the Bren right quick like – big fucking deal, he's still a wanker!'

Their banter was cut short by the sound of an Austin Champ Jeep and trucks driving slowly up the track toward them, 'That's the CO and RSM in that Champ,' Ronnie said as the vehicle stopped next to Lt Stanley who was standing to attention by the track. Climbing out of the front passenger seat, the CO, Lt Col Keith Proudlock acknowledged Lt Stanley's salute with a perfunctory wave of his right hand and turned to wait for the RSM and a young Captain to climb out of the rear. RSM John Jones or 'Jay Jay as he was known by the rank and file, although no-one dared call him that to his face, stood protectively behind his CO and turned to look as the young Captain in ill-fitting and almost new Olive Green jungle uniform stepped nervously forward.

Without looking at the nervous Captain, the CO addressed Lt Stanley, 'Sebastian this is Reggie Jerome from the Intelligence Wallahs; he has come to identify your bandits and take statements from your boys but first let me have a quick brief of events.'

Sebastian Stanley confidently briefed the CO on the ambush and highlighted Ronnie's part in the killing of the terrorist leader. The CO asked a few questions then accompanied by Jay Jay, he strolled over to where some of the soldiers of 2nd Platoon were resting. Raising his hand to indicate – 'don't get up,' he squatted next to his men and chatted to them informally about the ambush and how they felt on having completed their last jungle mission before returning to Singapore and back to the UK in September.

'We have a lot to do back in Singapore to ensure the barracks are ready for hand over to the Jocks but I'm sure the RSM and your CSMs will make sure we leave the place spick and span.' he said as he stood up.

Jay Jay grinned menacingly at the soldiers and said, 'Ye can be sure of that Sir!' He may have only been a wiry five foot ten but his ferocious demeanour more than made up for his lack of physical stature. Respected for his fair handed discipline, the 'Northumbrians' were planning a send-off befitting his rank and service in September when he was to be commissioned Lieutenant John Jones and replaced as RSM by Bill Armstrong, a different type of man altogether!

The CO then sought out Ronnie and called him and Fred over to one side for a chat, 'Lieutenant Stanley tells me that you bagged the top man Grundy and that you remained rock steady when he and another charged you?'

Ronnie felt himself blush but standing to attention he replied proudly if a little self-effacing, 'It wasn't ower hard like Sir, the two buggas just came running at me and I let them have it like!'

Smiling at the confident young soldier in front of him the CO said, 'Yes Grundy but from what I've been told they were firing a fair amount of rounds at you and you ignored that and did what was required.'

Fred interrupted, 'He did that Sir, those two were firing their SMGs straight at us but Jake here was as calm as oot and blasted the buggas Sir!'

'Sterling stuff the pair of you,' the CO said as he turned away, 'RSM give Grundy the news please.'

Jay Jay acknowledged with 'Sir,' before turning to Ronnie and Fred who remained standing to attention as the RSM said, 'Grundy, the Commanding Officer has decided that you should be rewarded for having topped the Big Baddy.'

Ronnie hid a smile and said, 'Thanks Sir, does that mean am getting the reward money?'

'No it most certainly does not lad, the Commanding Officer has decided to give you your stripe back, effective immediately, got that Lance Corporal Grundy?'

The promotion took Jake by surprise but he managed to splutter, 'Ta very much Sir.'

'Don't thank me lad, it was the CO not me, now get your kit together your platoon is moving back to join the Battalion.'

Pushing his bike around the sand dune, Ian was the first to see Jake and the carnage he had created. Stopping in his tracks he surveyed the scene slowly as Rafe, Howard and Roger joined him to stare incredulously at an *almost* embarrassed Jake.

Jake was lying flat out in a pair of red stained, grubby khaki shorts with an empty pop bottle and half demolished plate pie lying next to him along with a couple of opened parcels and tins but it was the scene behind that caught their attention; the tent canvas had disappeared and below the still upright poles someone had stacked their packs and neatly folded their sleeping bags, piling them on top of each other. They also saw the charred pieces of canvas dangling from the poles and the scorch marks and shreds that had been the bottom of their tent.

Ian was first to speak, 'What the blidy hell have ye done noo Jake, where's the tent?'

'I say, what a mess Jake my friend,' added tall, blonde and aristocratic looking, fourteen year old Rafe, Ian's uncle!

The insane grin that gangly, tousled haired Reg normally wore disappeared, something that rarely occurred as he looked at the remains of their tent, muttering, 'Good God Almighty!'

Big burly Howard dropped his bike in the sand and with his head lowered advanced menacingly toward Jake growling, 'That's it, I'm ganning te kill the skinny little git noo.'

The other three lads leapt on Howard and with some difficulty managed to restrain him as Jake sat up, belched loudly and let loose a slow rumbling fart, 'Aah had a bit of an accident but am alreet!'

'Accident! It looks as if a bomb has gone off man,' Ian said, 'your story better be good or we'll let Howard kill ye,' and looking at the empty pop bottle and half eaten plate pie, said, 'that better not be wore food that yor eating; has Mike been?'

'Grinning inanely, Jake replied, 'Aye Mike's been and Aah've just had a bite te eat cos Aah was starving man.'

Glaring at Jake, Ian snarled, 'Well what happened, I can see the stove where the tent was, divvint tell me that you lit that inside the tent?'

'Whey man Aah thowt it wud be alreet cos ye'd already used it and it was still primed like; hoo was Aah supposed te kna that the blidy thing wud explode!'

As Ian continued to grill Jake, Howard knelt down and quickly checked to see what food Mike had brought before he rose and confronted Jake angrily,' Where's the blidy filling oot of that pie?'

Jake tried to back off but Howard grabbed his arm and spat, 'Well?'

'Whey man Aah ate it didna, Aah was blidy starving man.'

Howard growled, 'So ye ate half the pie and the filling oot the other side?'

Before Jake could answer, Roger picked up an empty plate Jake had stuffed behind a pack and said, 'Look at this, tha must hev been a pie on here as weell, he's eating two frigging pies the greedy swine!'

Turning to look at the plate, Howard inadvertently released his grip on Jake's arm, allowing him to turn and sprint off across the dunes. Howard started after him but Ian called him back, 'Let him go Howard man, we'll sort the bugga oot later, let's see what the greedy sod's left.'

Chapter 2
A Returning Threat

Earlier in that morning, short, stout and with a huge heart and caring soul, forty-eight year-old Aggie Galloway or the Gallowa as she was affectionately called by everyone who knew her, was peeling potatoes at her table in the kitchen of number 49 of the unimaginatively named, 'Sixth Row.'

The Rows, or 'Ra's' were terraced miner's houses running in long straight lines in two groups parallel to High Market and Middlemarket of Ashington up to the huge and sprawling colliery, First to Sixth and Seventh to Eleventh Rows. The outside toilets, coalhouses and air-raid shelters of the Sixth Row backed onto the colliery shunting yards beyond which the new NCB Area Workshops that was currently under construction marked the edge of smoky Ashington and the beginning of the glorious Northumberland countryside.

A black car driving slowly past her window caught Aggie's eye and dropping the knife and the potato she had been peeling, she scurried to her back door and out into the small back yard just in time to see a battered 1946 Ford Prefect come to a halt at the end of the Row where two men she knew to be the local petty-criminals the McArdle twins, climbed out and looked around before entering the yard of number Fifty, the end house of the terrace, the house where until a few weeks ago Jane Trevelyan had lived with her children and drunken husband.

The thirty-year old swarthy skinned, dark haired McArdles fancied themselves as gangsters and modelled themselves on the many hoodlums they had seen at the cinema in Ireland when they were youngsters. Dressed almost identically in navy-blue double breasted suits, white shirts and garish ties, hair slick backed with pomade, they completed the look with grey fedoras worn at a slight angle and tipped forward to enhance their menacing appearance. They were there to collect gambling money owed them by the recently executed Nick Shepherd, money they had tried to collect from his widow before but had been bundled out of the street by the hard working, no-nonsense coal miners who lived there. They had chosen to try again at eight o'clock on a Thursday morning, hoping all the men in the street would be at work.

As Aggie stood silently straining to listen, the McArdles knocked loudly on the door of number 50 and stepped up close, waiting for it to be opened, intent on pushing their way inside and confronting Jane Shepherd/Trevelyan. The two men began to push the door open when they heard it being unlocked from the inside; Pat McArdle placing his foot quickly inside the door but stopped when he saw the frightened face of a wide-mouthed slightly awkward looking young girl!

Glaring down at the girl he demanded in his mix of Irish brogue and Geordie, 'Now who would you be then girl?'

'Holding tightly onto the door the auburn haired girl who was wearing a red gingham dress replied nervously, 'Am Julia, me Mam and Dad are at work, what de ye want?

Joe McArdle Stepped forward and asked, 'If yer Dad's at work he cannit be Nick Shepherd seeing as how they hung him a few weeks ago!'

Trying unsuccessfully to push the door closed, the now very frightened but unflinching girl answered, 'The Shepherds divvint live here anymore, my name is Compton, we moved in here three weeks ago.'

Pat stepped back from the door and attempting to smile pleasantly, sneered horribly at Julia, 'We're sorry Pet, it's Mrs Shepherd we've come to see, can ye tell us where she moved to?'

Hearing the question, Aggie sprang forward to try and stop Julia replying but she was just too late as Julia answered, 'Mrs Trevelyan ye mean, she's moved to Hotspur Hoose in High Market.'

Bustling into the yard, Aggie brushed past the McArdles and gently pushed Julia back into her house before rounding on the startled McArdles. 'Right noo ye two buggas can be on yer way right noo, the men folk around here hev already warned ye te stay away and like the wasters that ye are, ye come sneaking aroond when they are aall at work, whey we're not afeared of ye two nasty buggas noo go on before Aah call for the Polis!'

Joe McArdle glared menacingly at Aggie and taking a silver dollar from his waistcoat pocket, began tumbling it slowly between his fingers, mimicking a gangster he had seen in a film and growled, 'We're off now Missus, there's nothing here of interest to us now so just calm yerself doon,' then stepped out of the yard and climbed back into the Ford as Pat walked around to the driver's side. Sneering at Aggie, he climbed aboard, turned the car round and drove slowly out of the street.

Aggie turned back to the now terrified Julia and wrapping her arm around her shoulder led her back into the kitchen of the three up and two down end of terrace house, 'Sit yersell doon by the fire bonny lass and I'll mek ye a nice cup of tea and divvint worry aboot them two bad buggas, Aah divvint think they'll be roond here again, it's not ye or yor family tha want.'

After making a pot of tea and handing Julia a cup, Aggie said, 'Ah've got te gan and see Jane and tell her what's happened, noo ye lock the door till Aah get back but ye've nowt to worry aboot noo Pet.' Julia was worried though and locked and bolted the back door after Aggie left before wiping a tear from her eye as she walked back to the fireside chair and her cup of tea. What with a spot of bullying at her old School and now this, she was upset but such was her character that she said aloud, 'Whey am not ganning te be scared or bullied anymore – Aah'll lurn Judo or sumat and bash anybody up that bothers me again.'

The McArdles drove slowly along to the end of the Fifth Row, down Cross Row and turned left onto Ellington Road and the left toward High Market, parking outside the red bricked, Victorian built, Bothal School. Climbing out, they walked briskly to Gibson's Garage where Pat stopped and pointed to a sleek 1951, One point Five, red Riley saloon, 'Look Joe me lad, there's Nick's car, repaired and looking as good as new, now I wonder what it's doing here?'

Walking over to the car, Joe took out his silver dollar and began tumbling it through his fingers again and said, 'The garage must have repossessed it, seeing how Nick was hung when he probably owed money on it.'

Pat nodded and grinning evilly, snorted, 'Whey we have taken over his little gambling racket we might as well have his flash car as well.'

Joe turned and continuing into High Market said, 'But first his beautiful widow needs to cough up the money he owed us!'

It had been just after eight a.m. when Jane, dropped Tommy off at the house where her pretty but very heavily pregnant daughter Maureen lived in Wansbeck Road overlooking the copse that hid People's Park from the road.

Patting Maureen's now huge bump, she had asked, 'Did she keep you awake last night Pet?'

'*HE* did Mam, he's got a kick like a mule, he nearly kicked Terry out of bed.'

Smiling Jane asked, 'How is Terry, are his wounds totally healed now?

Maureen's face clouded as she remembered the dreadful day when her drunken father had stabbed her then boyfriend before fleeing and later murdering a Police Constable, 'Yes they have Mam, he says he has forgotten they are there now.'

'That's good to hear,' Jane said before turning to Tommy who had taken a seat at the kitchen table and picked up a slice of buttered toast Maureen had prepared for him, 'I'll see you later Tommy and make sure you behave yourself for Maureen.'

Tommy nodded and spluttered through a mouthful of toast, 'Yes Mam but am ganning roond te the Sixth Ra te play with Roger and Billy later on this morning.'

Jane's face tightened slightly, remembering how she had nearly lost Tommy and Ian in the New Moor bog, partly because of the actions of the two younger Grundy boys, 'Okay,' she said but no going over the 'Rec' and into the fields and make sure you call in at the Bakery at twelve and I'll give you something for lunch.

Walking the four hundred yards back to High Market, the close fitting plain pale blue dress she was wearing showed her slim but curvaceous figure to best advantage and the gentle August breeze ruffled her long black hair as she hurried back through the small copse that separated High Market from the Holy Sepulchre Church. She intended to pick up her white cotton dust coat from home before walking the 75 yards to Kirkup's Bakery but as she approached Hotspur House she could see Aggie looking flushed and nervous, hovering at her gate!

Hurrying up to her, Jane asked in her still refined accent, 'Whatever is the Matter Aggie, you look as if you have run a mile?'

'Eeee, Aah hev that Pet,' gasped Aggie as she sought to control her pumping heart and heaving lungs, 'them wicked buggas hev been to yor owld hoose looking for you!'

'Take your time please Aggie, what wicked 'buggas' are you talking about?'

Pausing to take a deep breath, Aggie placed her hand on her heaving bosoms as if to slow down her breathing and said staccato like,

'The McArdles - those wicked buggas – they hev been te yer owld hoose – looking for ye – the poor wee lassie there – telt them where ye live!'

Jane's beautiful face clouded as she looked over Aggie's shoulder, 'Thanks Aggie, it looks as if you just beat them here, there they are standing over by the bus stop watching us.'

Turning swiftly around Aggie, glared at the McArdles, who were leaning nonchalantly against the brick wall of the front gardens of the First Row just fifty yards away on the otherside of the road.

Almost shouting, Aggie spat, 'Ye nasty buggas ye, ye betta clear of cos we are ganna call the Polis.'

The sight of the McArdles upset and even frightened Jane but she managed to keep control and placing both hands on Aggie's shoulders, she gently steered her angry friend into her porch and quickly unlocking the door, she took her inside to calm down.

Inside Jane knew exactly how to soothe her visibly shaking ex-neighbour and said quietly, 'Aggie will you please put the kettle on for a cup of tea while I get my dust coat and look to see if they are still across the road.'

Smiling nervously, Aggie scuttled of to the kitchen as Jane grabbed her white work coat from the hooks in the rear porch and quietly climbed the stairs to look out of her bedroom window. The McArdles were still there and had obviously seen Jane looking down at them as Joe looked straight at her with a menacing grin spread across his chubby evil face, tugged the front of his hat and pointed his finger, gun like at her.

Shocked by his brazen implied threat, Jane stepped back from the window to consider her options; should she call the Police but what could she tell them? She could call Detective Sergeant Norman, the dishevelled but handsome Scot's Detective who clearly was smitten by Jane, he had told her to call him if the McArdles ever bothered her again but they could be just waiting for a bus! She could call the ever reliable Edward Thompson, the man she had grown very close to but again what would she say.

Aggie's shout of, 'The kettle's boiled Jane,' interrupted her thoughts and she turned to go back downstairs but stopped to have another look to see if the McArdles were still there. A red 'United' bus was just pulling away from the bus stop and as it moved forward she saw that the McArdles were gone!

'Maybe they had just been waiting for a bus, maybe Aggie misunderstood why they were there,' she thought as she walked down to join her dear friend in the neat, blue and cream painted kitchen, 'They've gone Aggie, I think they were just waiting for a bus?'

Although she was only ten years older than Jane, Aggie was almost a surrogate mother to her and was very protective of her and her children.

Pouring the freshly made tea, she shook her head and said fretfully, 'I divvint think ye've seen the last of them Bonny Lass, Aah think ye shud tell that scruffy Scotchy Polis what's ganning on.'

Smiling nervously, Jane said, 'We'll have to see if they come back before I can do that Aggie, now I haven't really time to drink the tea but please you sit there and have yours and pull the door shut when you leave, I've got to get off to work or Alice will be after me!'

Stopping to look in the mirror hanging in the spacious hall, Jane flicked her hair back with her right hand and breathed a sigh of relief before hurrying out the front door, turning left and walking a few paces straight into the McArdles who stepped out of the drive of the next door house!

'There you are now Missus Shepherd, so pleased to see you again,' Joe sneered as he and his brother blocked the pavement.

Jane tried to walk past but the two short but burly brothers moved, preventing her from passing as Pat said, 'Just a wee moment of your time Missus – we see that you must have come into some money now, seeing as how yer living in such a grand house.'

Joe continued the twin's double act by grabbing Jane's arm tightly and snarling, 'Right now that ye've got money you won't mind paying us the five hundred pounds your late husband owes us!'

Trying unsuccessfully to wrench her arm free of Joe's grasp, Jane snapped, 'You will get nothing from me but the police knocking on your door and, my husband owed you three hundred and eighty pounds not five hundred, not that you will get any of it from me.'

Joe released her arm and as Jane hurried past he took out his silver dollar and began twiddling it and growled, 'Interest Mrs Shepherd and it's increasing every day but we can take a wee bit of that lovely body of yours as part payment.'

Pat shouted after Jane, 'We'll be seeing you Missus,' as she stepped quickly into Kirkup's shop and stood inside shaking with fright.

Big, buxom, homely and flour covered Alice Kirkup looked at Jane and asked worriedly, 'My God Jane what on urth's the matter?'

Jane looked out the window and saw the McArdles on the other side of the road, strolling nonchalantly back to toward Bothal School and their car and replied, 'Something from Nick's past has just came back to haunt me.'

Chapter Three
Mary

Taking a couple of Capstan cigarettes out of the battered tin he carried them in, Fred Keating sat down heavily on the wooden bench seat of the open topped three-ton truck that was to take him, Ronnie, Harry and twelve other members of Two Platoon to the jungle airstrip where they would spend the night before the long journey down the Malayan Peninsular to their barracks in Singapore.

Handing one of the cigarettes to Harry, he lit his own before saying out loud, 'Whey that's us oot of the blidy jungle for the last fucking time, thank Christ for that man!'

Sitting next to him, Ronnie smiled and said, 'Aah didn't mind the jungle man, not once ye got used to it.'

Fred glared at Ronnie and said smiling, 'Ye've only been here since January man, that's just eight months, ye've hardly had time te get a blidy sun tan. Mind ye, ye hev managed te get blidy married to that gorgeous Chinky lass of yours!'

Frowning Harry asked, 'Aah thowt ye'd been here with the Battalion since fifty six Ronnie?'

As the vehicles drove slowly off along the rough and narrow jungle track, Ronnie replied, 'Nur man, Aah was in Second Battalion in Minden in Gurmany when they disbanded, the regulars wor given the option of joining Forst Battalion here, so I signed on for nine years and came oot here in December last year by an Airworks Hermes plane, it took us fower blidy days te get here man.'

Blowing a cloud of fag smoke at Harry, Fred said, 'We came oot by troopship and the battalions ganging back by troopship and that teks three lang weeks, a blidy nightmare, unless like this jammy bugga, ye can get on the Advance Party cos they're flying back!'

Harry looked enviously at Ronnie and asked, 'Hoo did ye get on the Advance Party then Ronnie?'

'Easy, they wor asking for volunteers so I put me name forward thinking that me and Mary would fly back together so I was a bit pissed off when Big Bill towld me that I was ganning on the Advance Party but me Mrs couldn't which Aah thowt was wrang.'

Fred interrupted, 'Aye so she's buying a ticket to fly back by BAOC, yor missus must hev some money to be able te afford that Ronnie lad.'

'Whey if she has, she hasn't towld me!' Then leaning against Fred, he pulled his battered cotton Jungle hat over his eyes and said quietly, 'Me Mam and Dad think am still in Gurmany and I hevn't telt them am married or signed on the regulars yet man, I've just sent them a letter last week telling them that I'm coming home on leave!'

Closing his eyes he cast his mind back to the January morning when he and the twenty other lads from the 2nd Battalion had joined the 1st Battalion at Nee Soon Barracks in the northern part of Singapore. The first day had been a whirlwind of kit issues and briefings including being told that they would have three weeks with their Companies to acclimatise before they would travel across the Causeway joining Singapore to Malaya to carry out three weeks Jungle Training in Johore Bahru.

At the end of the first busy day in the white painted colonial style barracks, Ronnie found himself allocated to Two Platoon and allocated a bed space in a first floor, eight man room cooled by two massive ceiling fans that spun non-stop. Two sets of double louvered doors opened onto a spacious balcony that ran around the three story building that had the Company offices and stores on the ground floor with accommodation on the two upper floors and the ablutions at the rear of the block.

Fred Keating slept in the same room and when he recognised Ronnie as a lad he had known at Bothal School, he was quick to take him under his wing, 'Right Ronnie Marra, tonight am ganning te introduce ye te the delights of the Lion Bar and a bit of 'Jiggy-Jiggy!' The Lion Bar was one of several Chinese run bars sprinkled amongst tailors, tawdry gift shops and fowl smelling Chinese and Malaysian food shops that lined the road outside the barracks.

Just after eight o'clock, Fred and two other lads took Ronnie to the NAAFI bar for a couple of pints before heading out of camp and down to the Lion Bar that was easy to spot due of the huge Lion painted on an enormous faded Metal sign that covered two windows on the first floor.

Looking up at the painted lion, Ronnie asked, 'That supposed to be a British lion?'

Grabbing him round the shoulders, Fred laughed, 'Ner marra, that's a Singapore lion, this is the 'Lion City' man!'

The 'Lion Bar' was long and quite narrow with a Formica clad bar running down the right hand side while on the left were several groups of Formica topped tables and chairs, nearly all of which were occupied by other soldiers. Most of the light was provided by the brightly lit bar supplemented by candles burning in small red jars on the tables as several large ceiling fans stirred the air in an effort to cool the occupants who were there for two things, booze and if they had enough money, 'Jiggy-Jiggy.'

Fred led the way to one of two empty tables at the far end of the room next to two doors, one with a badly painted 'Gents' sign and the other with an equally badly painted 'Private' sign. Within seconds of sitting down, a small Chinese girl wearing a very tight, short red dress with splits up to the hips appeared at the table and asked through a forced smile, 'What you drink boys?' The girl must have been in her early twenties and was very pretty in a tough way; Ronnie felt strangely intimidated by her.

'Four beers please Rose,' Fred said with the familiarity of a regular customer.

Rose put her arm around Fred's shoulder and kissing him on the cheek, asked, 'You not want buy me Champagne and I sit with you Fleddie?'

Fred pushed her away and gently smacked her curvaceous behind, retorting, 'Aah canna afford yor blidy shampoo man, I need te save me money for a Jiggy-Jiggy!'

Sipping the ice cold 'Tiger' beer, Ronnie enjoyed the banter at the table whilst noticing the occasional soldier and Chinese waitress disappear through the door marked 'Private!'

Wiping froth from his upper lip he asked, 'Fred why are the blokes and waitress ganning into the private room?' Fred looked at Ronnie with open-mouthed incredulity before bursting out laughing along with the other two as Ronnie looked on bewildered.

Just managing to control his laughter as one of the soldiers came back through the private door, Fred snorted, 'Ronnie lad they are hostesses not waitresses man!'

Still confused, Ronnie asked, 'What's the difference?'

Fred put his arm around Ronnie's shoulders and said, 'Bugga me, ye really hevn't got a fucking clue hev ye – waitress wait on, hostesses host and here that includes a bit of Jiggy-Jiggy upstairs for paying customers!'

Ronnie burst out, 'Blidy hell wa in a frigging brothel!'

'No man it's a just a Bar that provides a bit extra,' Fred said.

Two 'Hostesses' joined them and within a few minutes the three other lads disappeared through the 'Private door with the two girls as Ronnie sat drinking nervously on his own. After a few minutes another

Chinese girl appeared at his table but there was something different about this one, stunningly beautiful and wearing a traditional longer red Chinese dress with small discreet slits at the hem, she looked no older than him.

'What's the matter, you not want to have Jiggy-jiggy soldier?'

The words coming from such a beautiful and almost innocent face embarrassed Ronnie and he felt himself blushing fiercely as he grabbed his beer as though it would protect him from this brazen but gorgeous girl, 'No thanks, Aah divvint want te Jiggy-Jiggy,' he blurted.

'What the matter, don't you like girls?'

Blushing even more as the beautiful girl leaned on the table he replied, 'Aye, Aah think they are lovely like, Aah just divvint thing it's right te be paying for, for, ye kna, that em Jiggy-Jiggy stuff.'

'I get it, you prefer nice boy, sorry no boys here.'

Ronnie was aghast, 'No man, Aah divvint like boys, I like wimin man!'

The girl was beginning to enjoy herself with the shy and awkward Ronnie, 'Why you call me 'Man?' I'm not a man, we have no lady boys here, only women here.'

'Aah can see that man, sorry, I mean miss, man is just an expression we Geordies say man!'

Smiling the girl said, 'Lots of Geordies come here; you don't speak proper English, very hard to know what you say.'

Ronnie was stricken by the girls looks and disarming smile and wondered why she did what he thought she did and meekly said, 'Am sorry, it's me forst night here and I've just come for a drink like, Aah divvint want te Jiggy-Jiggy, not that Aah divvint like wimin and I think you are beautiful and would be lovely to Jiggy-Jigg, Aah just divvint think it's right like but if Aah did Aah would want te Jiggy-Jiggy with you!'

A frown crossed the girl's face and she spat angrily, 'You never bludy Jiggy-Jiggy me soldier, I not hostess, do you not know who I am?'

The outburst shocked Ronnie, 'Am sorry, I thought you were an em - sorry I don't know who you are.'

Calming down she said, 'I Mary Peng, this is my Bar - my brother and my Bar, I'm not hostess, Okay.'

Flummoxed, Ronnie looked shyly at the beautiful Mary and said, I'm very sorry if Aah offended ye Mary, Aah didn't mean to be rude, can Aah buy you a drink please to say am really sorry?'

She smiled and sat down next to him asking, 'What is your name soldier?'

'Ronnie, I'm Ronnie, clumsy, stupid, Ronnie who is very sorry for being a berk!'

Studying Ronnie's fine-looking face for any signs of mirth, she said, 'I buy you a drink Ronnie, it's from me to say welcome to the Lion Bar now you tell me about where you from.'

When Fred and the two other lads returned from their foray upstairs, they were gobsmacked to see Ronnie deep in animated conversation with the beautiful but strictly 'Out of Bounds' Mary and not wanting to interrupt sat at another table, especially as her older and very protective brother was watching Ronnie's every move with an unflinching glare!

Ronnie became a regular at the Lion Bar; every off duty night he walked down Transit Road, past the gift shops and tailors and into the Lion Bar where he took up post at a corner table that became 'Ronnie's Table' where he would spend the night chatting to Mary whenever she could join him while he drank one or two beers 'on the house,' much to the envy of the other soldiers who had to pay the inflated Bar prices for their drinks. He never went for a 'Jiggy-Jiggy' and although the hostesses always greeted him with huge smiles and greetings of 'Hallo Lonnie,' none of them ever approached him, he was strictly 'Out of Bounds' to them.

By May Ronnie had excelled himself at Jungle training, had been promoted to Lance Corporal (LCpl), had been on several anti-terrorist patrols in Malaya and was madly in love with the beautiful Mary whom he was yet to kiss. During their nights sitting together, they talked for hours slowly getting to know all about each other.

Mary told Ronnie of the tragic events of the Second World War when both her parents had been clerks at the British Military Hospital and had watched the Japanese soldiers butcher their way through the sprawling building, bayoneting sick and wounded soldiers in their hospital beds, raping nurses and bayoneting anyone who tried to stop them. Mary's Parents were eventually cornered in their office where her father was clubbed to death as her mother was forced to watch before she was raped and dragged off to join several other young Chinese girls who were all forced to become prostitutes for the Japanese Air Force. After several months, the Japanese made Mary a type of Madam for twenty or more of the other unfortunate girls, many of whom died during their three year ordeal.

Mary and her brother had been taken in by their Grandparents who owned a small tailoring business on the road outside Nee Soon Camp and were forced to watch when a few months later the Japanese hung their Grandfather for being a British Lackey! They only saw their mother four times during the occupation during which time their Grandmother's health declined leaving her bedridden by 1946 until 1950 when she passed away. Some of the girls who Mary's mother had been responsible for, looked to her for help after the Japanese surrender and when she decided to convert her parent's tailor's shop into a Bar, several joined her to become hostesses for the returning British and Australian

Troops. Mary's mother had died in 1956 leaving the Bar to John and Mary.

Ronnie told Mary of Ashington and how it was a small town that had been built up to support the ever expanding coal mine that opened in the 1850s. She had some problem grasping the fact that he came from a poor background and giggled when he told her of outside netties and baths in front of coal fires; 'I'm not bathing in tin bucket in front of fire where everybody see me,' she said with a twinkle in her eye.

After weeks of deliberating and worrying on how to move forward without ruining their relationship, he eventually picked up the courage to ask her out.

'Mary,' he said across the table early on a Wednesday night in late May, 'can I take you out to dinner?'

She loved the way Ronnie had dropped a lot of the strange Geordie words he had used when they first met while still retaining the almost musical lilt to his voice, 'Take me out to dinner Ronnie, I never have time to go out to dinner, I run this place with my brother.'

He was not about to give up and asked hopefully, 'Surely John can run the place on his own for one night Mary Pet, we have never been alone and I desperately want to kiss you.'

She blushed slightly but leant over and kissed him lightly on the cheek, 'I cannot go out with you without John saying so Ronnie.'

Then much to her surprise, Ronnie pushed back his chair and walked with a confidence he wasn't feeling, over to the bar where John Peng was in conversation with the barman.

Clearing his throat, he said a little too loudly, 'Excuse me John, can I talk to you please?'

John turned and slowly, almost contemptuously, looked Ronnie up and down before asking, 'What you want Ronnie?'

They had barely said a couple of dozen words to each other over the past four months as Ronnie suspected John was not happy with the situation between his younger sister and him but Ronnie took in a deep breath and asked, 'I would very much like your permission to take Mary out for dinner on Saturday night.'

John stared silently at him for what seemed like minutes before replying, 'Okay, but you be back here before ten 'o'clock,' and then turned back to the barman. Ronnie stared at his back for a second or two, he had expected at the very least an argument and was a little dumfounded as he walked back to join Mary with an inane grin spread across his face.

'He said Okay Mary!'

Smiling, she placed her hand on his and said quietly, 'That because you show him respect Ronnie,' she paused before leaning closer toward him and whispered, 'I like you very much Ronnie, I am looking forward to our date but there will be no Jiggy-Jiggy!'

Still not used to her innocent use of the occasional ribald phrase or word, he stifled a laugh and said, 'Of course not Mary.'

Having saved up a fair amount of his pay over the past few months, he was determined to take Mary somewhere nice for dinner, his mistake was asking Fred where to go, 'Tek hur to the Unicorn Restaurant Ronnie lad, they de brilliant steaks and it's reet posh, all the families gan there to eat man.' Not having seen much of Singapore, he took Fred's advice and arrived outside the Lion Bar by taxi at seven-o'clock to collect Mary.

There was no sign of her when he walked into the bar and worried that she might have changed her mind, he sought out John who said angrily, 'What you doing here, Mary wait for you at home?'

It had not occurred to him that she would be at home and didn't even know where that was and blustered, 'I'm sorry John, I don't know where you live.'

John shook his head and told Ronnie the address to give to the taxi driver before warning, 'Remember, Mary home by ten!'

Mary looked ravishing in a fitted white dress that showed her long black hair and stunning eyes off to perfection as Ronnie shyly handed her a small rose he had sought out that afternoon. She took the rose and kissed him on the cheek which released a swarm of butterflies in his stomach as she said, 'Thank you Ronnie, you look very handsome.' He was wearing a pair of newly made black trousers, a new and crisp white cotton long-sleeved shirt with a regimental tie and highly polished black Oxford shoes, all made especially for the night and all for a few Singaporean Dollars.

Opening the rear door of the black and yellow Morris Oxford Taxi, Ronnie waited until Mary had slid along the plastic covered leather seat, then climbing in after her, said to the taxi driver, 'The Unicorn Restaurant John.'

Mary took Ronnie's hand in hers and looking up at him, asked, 'Have you been to Unicorn before Ronnie?'

'No Pet but the lads say it's a really posh place!'

Mary looked disappointed but did not say anything!

A mile or more north of Nee Soon along the busy two lane road that passed an eclectic mix of houses and shops as well as a couple of paddy fields complete with wallowing water buffalo, the Unicorn was close to the sprawling British Naval Base and was used mainly by the families living on the large married quarters estate, and although it was clean, the food good and the service friendly enough, it was past its best and badly needed refurbishment but worse for Mary, she was the only none British or Australian customer there! She had expected that to be the case and prepared herself. When Ronnie opened the door she stepped confidently into the foyer and waited for him to join her. Ronnie took her arm and was about to lead her to a table but she gave him a look that stopped him and she said quietly, 'We wait until waiter show us to table Ronnie.'

Smiling at her he said, 'Oh do we, it's the forst time Aah've taken anyone te dinner so I didn't know like.'

The Head-Waiter, a short rotund Chinaman in immaculately white shirt and trousers came bustling over and bowed slightly to Mary and exchanged a few words as Ronnie said, 'Ye hev a table for Grundy please?'

The Head-Waiter nodded but turned and called over another waiter who he spoke to quickly in Mandarin before turning back to Ronnie and saying, 'Very sorry please Mr Grundy and Miss Peng, please have a seat for a moment and I give you drinks while your table prepared.'

Ronnie looked annoyed and demanded, 'I booked a table, why is it not ready man?'

Remaining calm, the Head- Waiter leaned forward and said quietly to Ronnie, 'The table they have for you not good enough, I prepare best table for you.'

Sipping the cold beer a waiter had brought, Ronnie could not take his eyes of Mary, she looked beautiful, poised and elegant as she took the tiniest of sips from a glass of lemonade, 'Why do you think they are giving us the best table Mary?'

She smiled at him and touching his hand, replied, 'Because you look so handsome and dignified Ronnie.' He believed her and sat up straight and cast a haughty look at the other diners as the Head-Waiter returned.

'Your table ready now, please follow me,' and he led the way through the crowded tables with Mary walking behind, her head held high as just about every pair of eyes in the room followed her, some admiringly, some jealously and one or two resentfully.

To Ronnie the night was the best he had in his life; their table was on a six inch platform set slightly back from the others and surrounded on two sides by imitation plants which afforded them just a little privacy. Mary was enchanting and they talked almost non-stop throughout the meal which, although well enough cooked, they hardly touched.

Standing on the porch of her elegant but faded colonial house on the edge of Nee Soon, Ronnie said, 'Aah've had the best time ever Mary Pet can I please take you out again?'

She nodded her head enthusiastically and replied, 'Yes Ronnie but next time, I choose bloody Restaurant!' She then lifted her head to let him know he could kiss her and taking her in his arms, he gave her a lingering, tender but passionate kiss before she stepped back and said, 'Thank you Ronnie for lovely night, I see you tomorrow,' and quickly unlocked her door and disappeared inside after blowing him a kiss.

A month later, after several more evenings together away from the Bar, Ronnie finally picked up the courage to tell Mary that he loved her to which she asked, 'So what you gonna do about it Ronnie, cos I luv you too?'

'Whey we'll get married and move into married quarters,' then his face clouded as he realised the importance of what he had just said before he continued, 'and you will come back to England with me?'

Mary frowned, 'What makes you think I can marry you, and why should I go to England?'

'Aah forgot about ye being Chinese, is tha some sort of funny religious ceremony or something like and Aah thowt ye'd like te gang to England Pet,' he said as his Geordie accent grew as his confidence faded.

Looking a little annoyed, she replied, 'The only funny religious ceremony is a Catholic wedding Ronnie, I am Catholic like you but you must ask John for his permission, he is head of house and I only want to go to England because I love you!'

John agreed but only after asking if Ronnie intended to take Mary with him when the Battalion left Singapore and warning 'Don't expect big dowry!' A dowry had never crossed Ronnie's mind and anyway, he wasn't at all sure what one was. Ronnie later found out that John was very keen to have Mary taken off his hands as he wanted to sell the Lion Bar and set up a new business in Singapore City.

A delighted Mary threw herself into wedding preparations, telling Ronnie, 'I organise everything, you just come with Best Man and two friends and no uniforms please!' They were married on Saturday 12 July 1958 in the Catholic Church in the village of Seletar next to the ever expanding RAF base and spent their honeymoon weekend at the Singapore Hilton where they both finally had a Jiggy-Jiggy.

At seven thirty on the Monday morning after the wedding, Ronnie was summoned to Big Bill's office where he stood nervously outside in his fatigue dress of navy blue PT shorts, boots with socks rolled down and beret, waiting to march in to the CSM's office.

Sandwiched between the OC's and the Company Office, Bill Armstrong's office contained only his desk and chair, a huge pin board with sheets of A4 orders and nominal rolls pinned to it and the ubiquitous spinning overhead fan, 'In here now Corporal Grundy he roared.

Ronnie marched in and slammed to attention in front of his CSM and said nervously, 'Sir?'

'There's a rumour going round that you got married at the weekend Corporal – to a Chinese girl, a Singaporean – Singapore National; tell me it's not true lad!'

Gulping and wondering what the problem was, Ronnie answered, 'Aah did Sir.'

Pushing his chair back, Bill stood up and glared down at the now terrified Ronnie, 'You haven't got a clue have you lad, not a bloody clue, ye cannot just go off and marry a non-British passport holder ye idiot, ye have to apply for permission, especially as presumably you will be wanting your new bloody wife to return to Blighty with you?'

'Yes I do, what have I got to do, will she need a new passport Sir?'

Bill looked up at the whirring fan and growled, 'Give me bloody strength, yes you will but first, you are 'Warned for Office' for marrying without permission and I'm sure there will be other charges that will cost you your stripe!'

Ronnie did lose his stripe but Big Bill and the Battalion Adjutant helped him process all the necessary paperwork and applications through the British High Commission and eight weeks later Mary was given a British Passport!

As the truck turned onto a tarmac road for the last couple of miles to the airfield, Ronnie remembered Mary's horror when she saw the 'Army Hiring' that had been allocated to Ronnie, one of many one bedroomed flats that the army rented from a Chinese local. 'We are not living here Ronnie, it tiny, you move in with me until we go to England,' she had ordered.

He now daydreamed of being with Mary in their huge bedroom in her old family home and wondered what she would make of his Mam and Dad's tiny two and a half up and two down house in the Sixth Row!

Chapter 4
A First Warning

Fearing that the burly Howard would 'masacree' him if he allowed him to get close, Jake snuck around the sand dunes and climbed stealthily to the top of the largest one over-looking their camp site and peered down at his pals below.

Opening the parcels that Jake had not ransacked, the four lads found the largest and heaviest one contained three tins of stewed steak, two tins of potatoes, a tin of mixed vegetables and a packet of Oxo cubes, 'It looks as if this is dinna tenight,' said Howard as he carefully stacked the tins by the primus stove which had at last been turned off.

'And there's a parcel here with sandwiches and fruit cake which Aggie must have sent,' Rafe declared, 'at least the rogue did not attack these!'

Ian took a sandwich and looking at the remains of the tent asked, 'Well what are we ganning te dee, kip under the stars or gan hyem this afternoon?'

Grinning inanely, Reg answered first, 'Aah want te stay here.'

Howard walked to the top of the sand dune sheltering the campsite from the sea and turning said, 'Aye me anall but forst am ganning te bury that skinny little git in the sand.'

Rafe added, 'Well that looks like that's settled, I'll make some tea to go with the sandwiches.'

The sound of Mike returning on his motorbike disturbed the quiet, Ian commenting unnecessarily, 'That'll be Mike back!'

Jake had seen Mike approaching and noticing that he appeared to be having difficulty riding the motorbike because of a bulky object strapped across the rear, he ran around the dunes to meet him, 'Yer back

Aah see, what's that on the back of yer bike?' he asked as Mike carefully dismounted, took off his helmet and goggles and began unfastening the object.

'It's a tarpaulin for you lot te sleep in tonight, I borrowed it from the men at the Boat shed,' Mike replied as he hoisted the bulky blue canvas tarpaulin on his shoulder.

Stepping forward, Jake asked, 'De ye want a hand te carry it?'

Giving him a withering look, Mike replied, 'Nur, stay oot the blidy way, yer nowt but a blidy walking disaster man!'

Distracted by Mike, Jake had failed to see Howard bearing down on him until the last moment but was too late to dodge him as Howard scooped him up and slammed him into the sand.

'Divvint kill him Howard, or if you really hev te, try to keep the spilt blood to a minimum,' Mike said as he carried the tarpaulin round the sand dune.

Straddling the frantically struggling Jake, Howard shouted over his shoulder, 'Am not ganning te kill the useless sod, am just ganning te brek every frigging bone is his skinny body!' Around by the tent the other three could hear Jake's screams as Howard picked him up and lifted him across his shoulders and followed Mike back to the camp.

Dropping the tarpaulin in front of the tent frame, Mike said, 'Ye can hoy this ower the frame and use it as a tent until ye go home, just mek sure Jake doesn't burn this doon as well.' Mike, Ian and Roger quickly threw the tarpaulin over the tent poles and secured it in place with the tent pegs as Rafe made a pot of tea and Howard dumped the still screaming Jake outside the tent and sat on him to prevent him running off.

'Am ganna be sick man, get of me blidy belly ye big fat bugga,' he pleaded as Howard slowly bounced up and down.

Ian came over and looking down asked, 'How are ye ganning te pay for the tent Jake, it's ganning te be thirty or forty quid?'

Howard stood up releasing Jake who sitting up to rub his stomach, replied pathetically, 'Aah cannit pay that much money canna, it was an accident man, ye'll hev te help me pay for it - please.'

He received a storm of 'Bugga offs and sod you,' from the lads along with various suggestions on how he could raise the money including 'Sell yer brain to scientists, tha'll niva have seen one made of shite before!'

It was Rafe who eventually said in his public-school drawl, 'Jake you really are an unmitigated disaster, you need to pull your socks up and sort yourself out, after all, I'm sure you don't want to be a buffoon all your life and please stop bleating over the tent, we had to insure it so there will just be a thirty bob administration fee to pay.'

'Thirty bob! Aah hevn't got thirty frigging bob man; Aah only mek ten bob a week on me paper roond.'

The lad's ignored his bleating and sat down to eat lunch, Howard smacking Jake's hand when he reached for a sandwich, snarling, 'Ye've had yors ye greedy little git, noo put a tee shirt on yer putting me off me sandwiches!'

An hour or so later, Mike had left for home and the Hacky Dortys were sitting round a small campfire nestled inside a circle of rocks and large pebbles, discussing their options on what to do for the rest of the day, Jake proposing, 'We can gan fishing doon at the harbour,'

Howard nudged him in the ribs and spat, '*We* did that this morning and if ye had of hev come with us, ye wouldn't hev a tent te pay for wud ye!'

It was Rafe who came up with the 'Idea,' 'I think that we the 'Hacky Dortys' should endeavour to spend the night in Bamburgh Castle, that would be terrific fun!'

Reg shook his head and said mockingly, 'That's stupid man, it closes at five so ye cannit spend the neet in there man!'

Ian agreed, 'Reg is right Rafe, we cannit spend the night there cos it closes and what for anyway?'

With a wry smile, Rafe replied, 'Yes I know it closes at five but I thought if we arrived there at four for the last hour we could all attempt to hide ourselves away and spend the night searching for the Pink Lady or the Armoured Knight, now that would be fun aye?'

'That soonds like fun te me,' Howard said before pointing to Jake and continuing, 'but if we dee try; this sacklass bugga here wud boon te get caught or cock it up for the rest of us man.'

Smiling, Rafe said, 'None of us might be able to hide away and anyway, he is small and pretty nimble and should stand a pretty good chance of hiding somewhere.'

Reg's permanent smile slipped and he asked with some concern, 'What happens if we do manage te hide in there, hoo do we get oot?'

'We explore the castle and wait until morning and come out after it opens,' answered Rafe.

Ian was first, 'I fancy a try at that.'

'Yes me too,' added Howard.

Reg shook his head, 'I'll stay here and look after the camp and wore bikes, am not spending the night in that spooky blidy place man!'

Rafe looked across at Jake who was pushing a piece of driftwood into the fire and asked, 'What about you Jake, are you game?'

'Whey aye man, champion, but who's ganna pay for me te gan in cos, Aah've got nee more money?'

'Ye niva have de ye, ye scrounging git,' Howard chided but added, 'Aah'll pay ye in.'

Back in Ashington, Just after twelve curly haired and cherubic faced eight year old Tommy along with thick set Billy Grundy and his younger brother Roger, whose National-Health wire framed specs were perched on the end of his beak like nose, walked into Kirkup's Bakery where Jane was serving a thin and pale looking lad.

Walking up to the lad, Tommy greeted him with, 'Hiya Den, fancy coming to the baths this afternoon?'

The lad looked at Tommy through sad eyes and said, 'Nur Aah canna gan in the baths cos the chlorine horts me ears, anyway am ganning te the Regal we wor Syd this afternoon te see the Dam busters again.' Nodding 'Hello' to the Grundy boys, he left the shop with a brown paper bag full of cream cakes as Jane handed a small bag each to her son and his two pals.

'Now Tommy,' she said, 'here's a pie each for your lunches and make sure you are home by three; have you had a good morning?'

Looking up at his mother, Tommy replied, 'Yes Mam, we've been playing footie in the Sixth Ra and then came straight here but a couple of men stopped us and asked us wor names.'

Jane's stomach did somersaults as Billy said, 'Aye the did but Aah telt them te sod off, me Mam towld us niva te speak to strange men and they looked right nasty like!'

Just managing to control her panic and with forced calmness, Jane asked, 'Where did this happen, are the men still there?'

Roger Grundy looked up at Jane and pushing his glasses back up his nose, said, 'In the First Row cut Mrs Trevlin,' his attempt at saying Trevelyan, 'tha waalking off doon the street noo.'

'Wait here boys,' Jane said as she stepped outside and looked down the road toward 'The White House Club' at the end of High Market where she saw the McArdles standing looking at her! Joe doffed his hat and the two men turned and walked into the plantation heading for the Portland Hotel where their car was parked.

Stepping back into the shop she grabbed Tommy and Roger's hands and said, 'Come on Billy we are going along to our house and I want you to stay there until Mike arrives home, Tommy will let you play with his train set won't you?'

Tommy nodded and Roger sniffed up his dew drop and said, 'Thanks a lot Mrs Trivlin.'

It's Tre-vel-yan,' Tommy corrected as Jane hurried the boys along to Hotspur House.

'That's whaat Aah sed man, Trivlin,' Roger replied, peeved at having been corrected.

Once home, Tommy led his two pals up to his bedroom as Jane rang Detective Sergeant Jamie Norman, the tall, bespectacled, good looking Scotsman who always looked as if he had just been pulled backwards through a hedge; the man who helped her during the aftermath of her late husband Nick's murderous drunken spree, the man she knew was besotted with her.

'DS Norman,' he said through a mouthful of cheese sandwich.

'Jamie it's Jane Trevelyan, the McArdles are back and they are demanding five hundred pounds but worse they stopped Tommy and his pals and asked their names, I'm sure they are trying to scare me and they are succeeding, I am terrified that they might hurt my boys...'

At the sound of Jane's voice, Jamie Norman dropped his sandwich and sat bolt upright and when she paused for breath he said in his soft Highland lilt, 'Calm down please Jane, now tell me, did they actually threaten you or your boys?'

'Well, no not actually threaten, more implied, they said they wanted five hundred pounds not the three hundred and eighty Nick owed them, that there was interest due and it was going up all the time, one of them actually suggested that I pay partly with my body!'

Jamie felt his anger rising at the thought of the two loathsome petty criminals intimidating the lovely Jane but he kept calm, 'Look Jane unless they have actually threatened you or hurt you in anyway, there's not much 'Uniform' can do but I will come round and warn them off if they are still about.'

Realising he was correct, Jane paused before saying, 'I think they have left for the time being but I would be eternally grateful if you could speak to them, I'm afraid to let young Tommy out on his own with those two about.'

'I don't think they would dare hurt you or your family, they are probably hoping that veiled threats will force you to hand over money to them but please don't do that, you owe them nothing; I will drive past later this afternoon to see if they are about and if not I will look again in the morning and will call into see you, is that okay?'

Felling a little calmer, Jane replied, 'Yes thanks Jamie I will see you tomorrow.'

'If they do reappear, just call me and I'll be straight around, see you tomorrow Jane.'

Placing the receiver back on the cradle, Jane flinched when she heard the kitchen door open and asked nervously, 'Who is it?'

'Just me Mam,' Mike shouted, 'I'm just back from Seahooses and another of Jake's calamities!' He was about to tell her of the tent fire but when he saw the worried look on his mother's face he asked, 'What on Earth's the matter Mam, you look as though you've seen a ghost?'

'I have,' Jane replied and sitting down at the kitchen table she told Mike of her brush with the McArdles and of them speaking to Tommy and the two Grundy boys.

Relaxing his tightly clenched teeth, Mike looked at his worried Mother and said, 'Look Mam it's all bluster, they wouldn't dare touch you or the kids, Aah think, tha just hoping te scare ye into given them money becos they think ye are soft ex-public school lass but hev ye told Sergeant Norman?'

'I was on the phone to him just before you arrived home, he says there's not much they can do unless they actually threaten or harm one of us but he will find them and warn them off. Tommy and the Grundy boys are upstairs, they want to go to the swimming baths but I'm afraid that the McArdles might still be about!"

Relieved that she had contacted the police, Mike said, 'Look I was going te spend the rest of my day off tinkering with my motor bike as it is misfiring a bit but I will take the lads to the baths so you can get back to work and divvint worry, I will look after them.'

Business had been improving steadily for clean cut, blonde and blue eyed Edward Thompson. Last year, the thirty-eight year old Electrician had set up his own and now successful business after having worked for the NCB since leaving the army as a sergeant in 1946. His distinguished war service had recently been recognised by the presentation of a Military Medal, a medal that had been mistakenly presented to the coward and drunken wife beater, his old school pal, Jane's husband Nick Shepherd, recently hung for the murder of a Police Officer.

Edward had won two large new contracts and as a result had taken on another electrician and a young trainee and was pleased with the way his business was progressing. If only he could say the same about his relationship with Jane whom he had been in love with since the first day he had seen her with her two oldest children in the Sixth Row back in 1944. He had been on a long weekend pass a few weeks before D Day and since then she had rarely been out of his thoughts even though she had been married to Nick.

He knew she cared for him but he was unsure if that was as a friend or if it was something stronger and although he had seen her and her children many times since the tragic events of May, he had not expressed his feelings for her nor had he asked her out; worried that it was too close to the death of her husband even though he knew she had stopped loving him many years ago and that in the end, she had felt only loathing for the drunken wife and child beater, turned murderer.

The telephone call he received just after lunch from Mike telling him of the return of the McArdles had angered him, he had thought that after he and the other men of the Sixth Row had chased the two thugs out of the Row that they wouldn't dare show their faces again. They were obviously far more arrogant and bolder than he had thought them to be! He told Mike that he would call in to see them all after work and that he would look out for the McArdles and perhaps have a word with them.

Edward was tall, well built and carried no fat and could look after himself in a scrap. He was not afraid of the McArdles but taking on two of them on his own was something not to be rushed into and needed some thought. One thing he was sure of, they had to be stopped from bothering Jane and her family and stopped for good.

The other man in Jane's life was the father of Mike's girlfriend Jennifer; Doctor Jonathan Metcalf of Morpeth. The distinguished looking forty-something widower had also fallen for Jane's classic beauty and well-bred manners and sure that she would be an asset to him, was setting a course to try and win her hand despite being well aware that Edward was in love with her. He knew he could provide Jane with something of the privileged life style she had been accustomed to before she had had to marry Nick back in 1940 and intended to use that to his advantage. He had already taken the first step and asked Jane to accompany him to the prestigious Mid-Northumberland Late Summer Ball on September the sixth at Alnwick Castle. Not having been to a Dance let alone a Ball since she was married, Jane had readily agreed and with some excitement had bought from Fenwick's of Newcastle, a stunning low cut, mauve ball gown that flattered her slim but shapely figure to perfection.

Unbeknown to Jane, Edward had acquired two tickets to the Ball from the Rotary Club and had been waiting for the right moment to ask her to partner him. Aware he was cutting it fine and knowing he could not wait any longer, he decided he would ask her when he called round to see her after work!

Just after five o'clock under darkening and stormy skies, DS Norman drove slowly past the eight Edwardian houses between the Whitehouse Club and Willington's Newsagents in High Market, slowing as he past the red Jowett Javelin parked behind Jane's Morris Traveller outside Hotspur House and then on past the eclectic mix of shops until he reached Gibson's Garage at the far end. Having not seen any sign of the McArdles, he turned to drive home unaware that the twins were sipping whisky with a ship's Engineer in their rundown, long, green caravan that sat squalidly amongst piles of scrap wood and iron and two derelict cars on an open but secluded area of scrub land on the south side of the estuary of the river Wansbeck overlooking North Seaton moorings. They had collected the Engineer from a ship that had berthed that in Blyth harbour that morning and were plying him with whisky as they discussed collecting the contraband he had on offer. Another lucrative illegal deal in the offing meant leaving their pursuit of cash from Jane until the following week.

In Hotspur House, as she laid the kitchen table, Jane asked Edward, 'You will stay for something to eat won't you?'

'I would love to Pet but only if I'm not robbing the lads of tha food,' he replied, relishing the idea of spending time in her company.

Smiling and touching his arm she replied, 'I have made enough for an army and there's only Mike, Tommy and me, so there's more than enough, if you want a beer help yourself to one in the pantry.'

Taking a bottle of Amber Ale from the crate in the pantry Edward decided that before her two boys came through from the sitting room where they were watching television, the time was right to ask Jane to the Ball.

Trying to be nonchalant, he asked, 'Jane, did you know the Mid-Northumberland Summer Ball was being held in Alnwick Castle?'

Taking the huge pan of mince and dumplings out of the oven where it had been cooking slowly, she placed it on the table and replied excitedly, 'Yes I did and Jonathan is taking me, I have already bought…..' she stopped realising that Edward had been about to ask her, 'Oh sorry Edward, I'm rattling on, have you got tickets?'

Crestfallen and just a bit annoyed, he replied, 'Yes, Aah'll see you there.'

Upset that she had probably disappointed him and that she had missed the opportunity to be in his company socially, she said, 'I'll save some dances for you then,' she was going to ask who he was taking but thought it might embarrass him.

'I'll look forward to that Jane but Aah doubt Aah can dance as well as the good Doctor,' he replied, already looking forward to holding her in his arms but first he had to find someone to take – the lovely Sandra perhaps? The divorced daughter and Secretary of his main electrical components supplier had made a play for him on more than one occasion!

Changing the subject quickly, he said, 'There was no sign of the McArdles when I drove around but if they do show their ugly mugs roond here again, just call me and Aah'll come straight over.'

Looking at his intense blue eyes, she thought for a moment before replying, 'I know you would Edward but I would rather let the Police handle them, I would hate for you to be hurt by them or become embroiled in some sort of trouble; they are just not worth it.'

Mike and Tommy burst in; stopping him from telling her that he would do anything to stop anyone from hurting or upsetting her, 'By that smells smashing Mam, tha's a right storm brewing outside,' Mike said, pulling back a chair at the table as a flash of lighting lit the room followed by the distant rumble of thunder.

Chapter Five
Frightening Storm

Just after four o'clock, the sun had been replaced by dark, foreboding clouds scurrying across the battlements of Bamburgh Castle as the Hacky Dortys, minus Reg, paid for their tickets at the entrance below the twin round towers of the East gate. Wearing jeans and jumpers in preparation for a long night, they were in high spirits as they hurried along behind the elderly and distinguished looking Guide who led the party of twenty or so holiday makers along a walled road and through square built Constable Tower. He steered them across the Inner-Ward and into the Museum that had been the original kitchens before being used as a girls' school in the 18th and 19th centuries.

Jake was finding it difficult to contain his excitement at the thought of spending the night in the huge castle, 'It's ganna be blidy brilliant and deed easy te hide somewhere cos it's massive man!'

'Shut up and stop jumping aboot, ye'll give the game away, now split up so he cannit keep track of us,' Ian warned as they moved around the exhibits with the guide droning on in a pseudo cultured voice in front. They followed on through a second smaller room before entering the enormous 'Great Hall' where the four of them stopped and looked up in awe at the massive 'Hammer and Beam' teak roof.

'That is some craftsmanship,' Rafe said admiring the work of Lord Armstrong and his Victorian builders who had renovated the castle at the end of the 19th Century. Ignoring the guide they then scuttled round the huge hall surreptitiously searching for somewhere to hide but despite its vast size, none of them were able to find a suitable spot.

Marshalling everyone into an untidy gaggle, the guide led them into the smaller 'Faire Chamber' that had been women's apartments and furnished accordingly. He then led them on through the long stone-walled passageway that led into the mighty Keep with its massively thick walls and into the arched roofed Armoury.

Ian and Jake examined a medieval suit of armour closely, both considering it as an option for hiding in but Ian turned to Jake and smiling, shook his head and said 'Nah!'

After a ten minute speech on the history of the Armoury, the Guide led the group along into the panelled, carpeted and comfortable 'Court Room' that had probably been the main Hall in Norman times. Try as they might, the boys could not find anywhere suitable to hide, besides which the Guide appeared to paying a lot more attention to them as he led them down the stone stairs, past the entrance to the dungeons and into the ground floor room with its massive arched and pillared ceiling and recessed slit windows high up in the walls on three sides.

The room was about forty foot long by twenty foot wide with two huge square pillars ten foot from each end that supported the arched roof. A half glazed oak door with massive chains hanging on either side led through to the scullery while a large stone fireplace occupied the corner to the left of the door through which they had entered. Various artefacts and weaponry adorned the walls including a buffalo head and knight's armour.

Forgetting why they were there, Howard stepped forward to exam another suit of armour standing on-guard inside a huge window recess and turned when Rafe nudged him asking, 'Where's Ian?'

'He's with Jake, isn't he?'

Rafe looked across at Jake who was paying a lot of attention to a huge old settle with a hinged seat over a storage box standing against the wall close to the half-glazed door but there was no sign of Ian.

Turning back to Howard he said, 'He must have found a hiding place somewhere as I can't see him, Jake is over there on his own.

Howard looked past Rafe, 'Where, I can't see him?'

Looking back at the settle, Rafe saw that Jake had also disappeared!

Sniggering he whispered, 'I think he's inside the settle, come on let's not draw attention to him.'

Unable to find anywhere to hide, Rafe and Howard dejectedly followed the Guide out of the Keep and into the Courtyard of the Inner-Ward into what appeared to be almost night; the storm clouds having stolen the sun while the North-East wind whipped storm clouds over the fortress.

A brilliant flash of lightning followed almost immediately by a mighty clap of thunder caused a few shrieks from the women in the group just as the rain began; not slowly nor as a shower, it was an instant deluge that hit them like a raging monsoon, scattering the group and sending them running for the nearest shelter; the Guide scuttling back inside the keep with half of his group.

Looking through the doorway at the torrent of rain sweeping across the courtyard he said reverently, 'My God that is Biblical Bloody rain, a real summer storm,' and as if to confirm his statement, another bolt of lightning hit the conductors on top of the Keep, the accompany thunderclap driving the group further inside.

Lying inside the six foot long storage box of the settle, the thunder was only a distant rumble to Jake as he eased his bony body on the age-hardened wood of the coffin-like compartment, 'Frigging ghosts and ghoulies are starting urly,' he whispered, unaware of the intensity of the storm raging outside.

The cleared strips of jungle on either side of red laterite airstrip that Jake's brother Ronnie and the rest of his company had debussed at two hours earlier was covered in a plethora of rapidly erected hootches illuminated by torches and lanterns as the soldiers endeavoured to make themselves comfortable for the night. A mobile bath unit had been set up at one end of the strip, priority for the showers being given to the Advance Party who would be leaving at five in the morning to drive into Kuala Lumpur to catch a train down to Singapore. Big Bill walked amongst his men ensuring the platoon commanders and sergeants had withdrawn all live ammunition and taken 'I have no live ammunition' declarations from their soldiers before he too headed for the tent he was going to spend the night in. He also needed a shower and was hoping to get a couple of hours sleep before ensuring the men in the Advance Party were ready to move at five.

Back at Bamburgh at a quarter-past five, the rain slowed to a downpour and the guide said in a loud and slightly annoyed voice, 'Ladies and Gentlemen, the Castle closed at five so I am going to have to ask you all to make your way to the main exit at the East Gate while I ensure the remainder of the group have left, thank you.'

The group of folk huddled in the stairwell reluctantly left their sanctuary and headed for the exit, some complaining whilst others made a dash for the exit before fleeing to their cars parked on the other side of the drawbridge. Rafe and Howard stopped briefly at the East Gate to see if there was any sign of Ian or Jake before Rafe sprinted off shouting, 'I'm freezing, have you any soap for our rain shower Howard?'

Stuffing his hands into his pockets, Howard hunched his shoulders, lowered his head and plodded out into the rain, across the draw bridge and into the sand-dunes for the half mile walk back to their tarpaulin tent!

When he had first climbed into the settle, Jake had lifted the lid carefully every five minutes or so for a peek but not having seen anything but the huge buffalo head staring angrily down at him, he settled back to wait and almost immediately fell asleep. Waking with a start an hour or so later he sat upright, smashing his forehead into the underneath of the heavy wooden seat of the settle and forgetting where he was, panicked and threw it open and tried to leap out but tripping on the high sides, he fell face first, banging his head for a second time but this time on the hard stone floor.

Kneeling up, clasping both hands to his bruised forehead, he remembered where he was and spat, 'Frigging blidy shite, that blidy hort man,' just as another flash of lightning illuminated his eerie surroundings, flashing of the polished suit of armour that appeared to be watching him malevolently!

'Bugga this,' he said nervously as the rumble of thunder reached him from the receding storm and leaping back into the sanctuary of the settle he closed the lid, trying to control his panicked breathing so that he could hear any approaching ghosts! As his breathing eased he rubbed his bruised head and tried to remember what Rafe had said about ghosts.

Thinking aloud, he whispered to himself, 'Tha's the Pink Lady, Aah remember him taalking aboot that one, noo whaat waas the other one?'

He remembered and almost shrieked, 'The Armoured frigging Knight, the blidy frigging Armoured Knight, Aah've just seen the bugga!'

He racked his brain, trying to remember if he had seen the suit of armour before he had climbed into the settle but his fear got the better of him – he let out a long rumbling, fart that instantly polluted the confined space with a vile stench that forced him to throw the lid open again as he quickly but nervously stepped out to breathe some relatively clean and unpolluted air and began backing quickly into the corner, his eyes never leaving the suit of armour.

Hunkering down, trying to be as inconspicuous as possible, he thought to him-self, 'Whose blidy bright idea was this? Am positive Aah saw that blidy suit of armour before I hid here, at least Aah think am positive, blidy shite man, Aah canna remember!'

As another storm raced across the North Sea with the castle firmly in its sights, Jake gained a little courage and slowly stood. Hugging the wall he moved carefully to his right, stepping gingerly past the large open fireplace that the wind whistled spookily down forcing him to quicken his pace toward the door. With his back to the door, his eyes still firmly on the shadowy figure of the Knight, he reached behind him and turned the handle of the large oak door – it was locked!

'Ur come on man, for fugg's sake let me oota here,' he pleaded but try as he might the door would not budge. Staring at the suit of armour until his eyes hurt, afraid that if he blinked it would leap on him, he shuffled off to his right again, intent on following the walls around until he was behind the knight - then he would fettle the blidy thing! Stepping around a large glass display case, he reached up and tried unsuccessfully to take a sword down from where it had been screwed across another and moaned angrily before he moved on to the table at the bottom of the hall where for the first time he took his eyes of the suit of armour to look up for another weapon.

And then to his horror, high on the end wall on either side of a narrow window, he saw two figures in the shadows staring down at him! He let out a strangled screech of, 'Fugging hell!' and backed up a few steps until his brain read the messages his eyes were sending him, 'It's ownly a couple of chain mail vests for fugg's sake!'

Jake began moving again and stepped slowly up to the back of the suit of armour, raising his hand to bravely touch it just as the second storm smashed against the shore at the foot of the castle and raced on, screaming over the battlements as it attempted to devour the mighty fortress, touching the tip of the lightning conductor on top of the keep with a flash of blinding light and an almighty clap of thunder!

Leaping into the air screaming with fright, he raced back into the corner opposite the paned-glass door, 'Mam,' he shrieked involuntary, crouching down trembling in the corner as several more lightning strikes lit the room and their thunderous accompaniment shook the very air, 'Blidy hell man get me oot of here!'

Still staring at the unmoving armour he felt something in his hand and looking down saw that he had somehow snatched a cutlass from the wall and was pointing the heavy weapon at the unmoving spectral shape in front of him.

Emboldened by the weapon in his hand he snarled, 'Reet ye Bugga ye, noo let's see if ye're a blidy ghost or not,' and slowly standing, he readied himself to once again sneak up on the armour but before he could step off, a ghostly light began to flash in the corridor behind the glazed door.

Backing into the corner, Jake moaned, 'Noo whaat? The frigging Pink Lady?'

The light danced of the walls, stopping occasionally when more flashes of lightening and claps of thunder disturbed its progress. Eventually the light played against the glass of the door and suddenly disappeared, leaving Jake trembling with fear. Realising he had stopped breathing, he gulped in a lungful of air just as the door slowly and silently began to swing open, revealing the shadowy outline of a huge hulking creature with one glowing red eye!

Jake held his breath again as the thing leant slightly to one side before shuffling into the room, its red eye pointing directly at him as it moved behind one of the pillars. Terrified, Jake decided to try and run around the other-side of the pillar and out the door before the huge shadowy monster trapped him. Raising the cutlass above his head and screaming at the top of his lungs he bolted for the door and barged straight into another, even taller shadowy monster that knocked the sword from his hand and grabbed him in a vice like grip!

    Reaching the tarpaulin tent ahead of Howard, Rafe stopped a few yards away to take in the scene as the first storm front slowly moved on. The tarpaulin was still securely pegged down on the side facing the wind but the other side had torn loose and was flapping wildly as Reg desperately clung onto a tent pole in an effort to stop their accommodation from being ripped to shreds. Rafe raced down and grabbing the flapping tarpaulin, struggled to hold it down and re-attach it to the tent pegs. The task would have been impossible if Howard had not arrived, enabling the three of them to secure the tarpaulin as the wind dropped a little.
    Soaked to the skin and shivering from the effects of the cold wind, the three lads looked at each other and their soaked packs and burst out laughing. Sniggering at their plight, Rafe asked Reg, 'What about our sleeping bags have they blown away?'
    Pointing to their bikes, Reg replied, 'No, I piled our bikes on top of them te stop them blowing away but tha aall soaked and Jake's blidy blanket took off like a kite so bugga knas where that is!'
    Seeing that Reg had wedged their box containing their provisions and cooking kit under the corner of tarpaulin and unaware of the second storm front racing toward them, Howard said, 'Howay, we'll mek a cuppa and hev sumat te eat, the storm seems te be dying doon.' Within minutes they had all opened their packs and pulled on just about all of their other clothes as the stove struggled to boil the kettle in the wind blowing in around the sides of the box.
    The second storm front raced over the beach lifting Ian, who had been making his way back to the tent, off his feet and threw him into the other three who had just stepped out to see what was happening. The

four lads fell back inside the open-ended tarpaulin as the wind increased; an almighty gust ripping the seam from the tarpaulin on one side. For the next five minutes the lads tried in vain to hold the tent together but the wind was still gaining in strength making the task impossible.

Ian screamed at the others, 'Take it doon; collapse it before it blows way, we cannit keep it up and we cannit stay here!'

Howard screamed back against the noise of the wind, 'What are we ganna dee?'

'Tek all the kit to the pillbox ower the sand dunes, we'll hev te spend the night there,' Ian yelled.

The next half hour was a nightmare! Soaked to the skin, battered by the wind that blasted sand at them, the four friends struggled to move the remains of the tarpaulin, their bikes and belongings the hundred yards to the World War Two concrete pillbox that was perched on the edge of the sand dunes still guarding the beach against the threat of invading Nazis! The inside was dark and a tad smelly but despite the wind howling through the front slit, it was mainly dry and the sand that had blown in over the years was soft. They left their bikes on the sheltered side of the pillbox as they attempted to make themselves as comfortable as possible in the almost dark interior and Howard once again set about making a brew.

Leaning close to Ian, Rafe shouted over the roar of the wind, 'What happened; we lost sight of you in the Keep at the same time that Jake climbed into a settle?'

Ian smiled and shouted his reply,' Aah went through the door next te the seat and doon some stairs into a big sort of kitchen or scullery. Aah looked around and found a big cupboard te hide in and stayed there for an hour or more but when Aah came oot for a look roond I walked straight into a couple of big security guards and they gave me a right telling off and hoyed me out! They didn't believe me when Aah said Aah was lost!'

Rafe nodded, 'That mean's Jake is in there on his own!'

Ian shouted, 'Aye, good luck to him, it's really spooky in there man; mind at least he will be dry!'

Screaming and struggling madly, Jake tried in vain to break the vice like grip that the tall monster held him in and expected to be devoured whole at any second but was instead blinded when someone switched the lights on!'

Squinting at the monster, Jake was shocked to see the face of a man who looked every bit as frightened as him, 'Jesus Christ lad ye scared the blidy shite oot of us,' the man snarled, 'hoo the hell did ye get in here?'

Still terrified, Jake stuttered, 'Get me oot of here man, the place is full of blidy ghosts!'

The tall man lowered Jake to the stone floor but did not release his grip on his shoulder and asked the hulking monster behind Jake, 'Whaat de ye think Harry, shall we lock this one up in the dungeons with the other little bugga we caught?'

Harry, Jake's one-eyed monster who turned out to be a huge bald headed Security guard with a limp and a glowing cigarette dangling from his bottom lip, shuffled over to Jake and glaring down at him, snarled, 'Aye Frank but forst let's try oot some of the tortures on the little sod and see if he lasts any longa than his marra, especially when we burn his eyes oot with the reed hot poker!'

Still not realising the two men were Security Guards, Jake moaned, 'Nur ye canna dee that man, it's not right!'

Gripping Jake tightly, Frank said, 'Of course we can, nee bugga knas yer here de tha?'

'Aye the dee, me marras kna and me Mam and Dad kna and me brothas kna, iviry body knas am here man, so ye canna de owt te me can yer.'

Taking hold of Jake's other arm in his pudding like hand, Harry growled, 'Aye we can unless ye tell us what the buggery ye were up to in here?'

'I'll tell ye iviry thing man just get me oot of here please,' Jake pleaded.

With what looked to Jake like a hideous maniacal grin, Frank said, 'Aye aall in gud time but forst we hev te hev a bit fun in the torture chamber with ye, Aah think we'll stretch ye on the rack forst!'

Dragging Jake to the door to the outside, Harry demanded, 'Noo whaat wore ye deeing in here lad?'

'Me and me friend wor just ganna see if we could hideaway and then look for ghosts but Aah've seen enough, Aah just want te gan please.'

Following on behind, Frank said, 'Forst we hev te decide whether te hand you ower te the polis for breaking and entering or burglary, or just torture ye for a couple of hours then hoy ye oot!'

Jake spluttered, 'I hevn't broken owt man and Aah didn't brek in, Aah was already in wasn't Aah so the police canna de owt can they?'

'Torture it is then,' Harry said as he swung open the massive door to the keep revealing to Jake just how ferocious the storm raging outside was.

Looking at the wind lashed rain racing across the courtyard, Jake declared, 'Blidy hell!'

'Aye it is,' Frank agreed, 'and we canna be bothered we paperwork so we have te get ye through that, doon te the gate and hoy ye oot!'

Jake flinched as another flash of lightning illuminated the courtyard and he sunk his head into his shoulder as the accompanying clap of thunder echoed round the fortress.

He pleaded 'Can Aah not wait here until the rain stops and hev ye got owt te eat cos am starving?'

Smacking Jake lightly on the back of the head, Frank snapped, 'Cheeky little bugga,'

A few minutes later, already soaked to the skin, Jake was unceremoniously pushed out the gate of the castle with 'Noo bugga off ye little waster ye!'

Earlier, as Jane, Edward, Mike and Tommy sat at the kitchen table eating their mince and dumplings, the frequency of the thunder and lightning increased as did the noise of the wind as it battered rain against the window.

Jane stood up and looked out at the storm darkened night and said worriedly, 'I do hope the boys will be alright in their tent tonight!'

Placing his knife and fork down, Mike said, 'Mam, I was going to tell you aboot their tent urlier but what with the bother with the McArdles Aah forgot!'

Turning to look at her son with a frown on her beautiful face, she asked, 'What bother Mike, what on earth are you talking about?'

'Jake Mam, he managed to burn the tent doon!'

With growing fear for the safety of her son and his friends she asked, 'My God is anyone hurt, are they all okay?'

'Aye they were all fine when Aah left them.' Mike told of how Jake had burned the tent down and how he had borrowed a tarpaulin for them and helped them secure it over the poles.

Edward who had been listening intently interrupted, 'This storm is in for the night and Aah doubt if a tarpaulin will stay up let alone keep them dry, Aah think we had better go and fetch them home Jane.'

Looking outside at the torrential wind driven rain, Jane turned back to Edward and said, I don't think I can drive though this storm Edward!'

'We'll need two cars to get them all home lass, so I'll lead in my car and you can follow behind with Mike, he'll have to come as he is the only one who knows where they're camping, but what about Tommy. You can't leave him here on his own?'

'Aah'll be alright on me own Mam,' Tommy ventured.

Jane touched his shoulder gently and said, 'No Pet, I'll drop you off at Aggie's and I can tell Jake and Howard's parents what we are doing as I'm sure they'll be worried.'

Edward added, 'Mike grab some blankets and I'll call in at the Proudlock's and tell them what's happening then, I'll meet you at Cross Row Jane.'

Twenty minutes later the two cars headed out along the Ellington road with their windscreen wipers working hard to clear the rain as it tried to batter the cars to a standstill. Edward leant forward and wiped the windscreen of his Jowett with the chamois he kept under his seat and said to himself, 'Keep it nice and slow, don't lose Jane.'

Jane's hands gripped the steering wheel of her Morris traveller tightly as she concentrated on keeping the lights of the Jowett in sight as Mike sat forward watching the road intently through the small area of windscreen cleared by the over worked wipers, 'It's ganna tek us a couple of hours te get there in this Mam,' he said.

The gale was playing with Jake, he was trying to run through the storm to the sanctuary of their tent but the wind kept on bowling him over and when he stood up it whisked him along at break neck speed, his legs hardly able to keep pace. His saturated jumper and jeans were both covered in clinging sand and weighed a ton and he was in danger of losing his battered baseball boots. The only way he could stop to tighten the laces was to throw him-self down behind a sand dune and quickly adjust them before the storm drove him on like a demented seagull flapping its wings as it tried to take off from a stormy sea.

The storm robbed him of his strength but pushed him on; forcing him onto his hands and knees to scale the large sand dune that hid their campsite from view. He tried to stand on the top but the wind picked him up and threw him down the other side where he rolled all the way to the bottom to lie in a sodden exhausted heap next to a few tent pegs; all that remained of their camp! Hauling himself onto his hands and knees and using one hand to protect his eyes from the wind and rain, he cast around for any sign of the tent and his friends.

Unable to see anything more than a broken tent pole and half a dozen tent pegs, panic set in, 'Blidy hell,' he thought, 'the frigging winds blown them away, tha'll aall be deed or knacked, tha probably frigging miles away hanging on te that shity tarpalin thingy, what the shit am a ganna dee?'

Fearing that his pals were all either dead or injured, he knew it was up to him to seek help, the nearest being in Bamburgh but first he had a hundred yards of sand dunes to cross and the wind was even stronger than before! He rested for a second or two then hauled himself upright and allowed the wind to blow him up and over the first sand dune and on to the next one. Holding his arms out in an effort to balance his speedy forward wind-blown momentum, he wind-milled his way out of the sand dunes and onto the stretch of coarse grass that separated them from the Seahouses to Bamburgh road where he tried in vain to steer himself into the wind toward Bamburgh. The wind was not having that and forced him south east, throwing him painfully onto the wire fence at the road side.

Realising he was not going to be able to battle the wind the half mile to Bamburgh he turned south and let the wind and rain hurry him the mile or so down to Seahouses and help.

The drive from Ashington was nightmarish; trees blown over by the gales forced Edward and Jane to detour through Alnwick before heading across to Seahouses. Driving into the face of the storm left vision down to a few feet as the wipers were unable to cope with the amount of rain thrown at them but they eventually reached the fishing village that appeared to be deserted as everyone took shelter from the storm. Constantly checking in his rear view mirror to ensure Jane was close behind him; Edward drove slowly out of the village and headed along the almost straight road north to Bamburgh.

Peering into the rain he was startled to see a wild figure with arms flailing madly, hurtling down the middle of the road straight toward him! He braked carefully not wanting Jane to crash into his rear as the figure glanced off the bonnet of his car and was whisked on past by the gale leaving Edward with a fleeting glimpse of Jake's panic stricken and exhausted face.

Leaping out of the car straight into the teeth of the gale, Edward hurtled past a startled Jane as he sped after the out of control Jake catching him and knocking him into the verge after a hundred yard wind assisted sprint!

Lying half on top of the exhausted Jake, Edward slowly turned him over and was shocked at the sight of the lad's bewildered face and shouted, 'Jake, Jake, it's me Edward Thompson, are ye alright lad, where's the rest of the boys?'

Recognising Edward, Jake was engulfed with relief and began crying as he spluttered, 'Tha gone, tha aall gone, the wind's blaaing them away te buggary, Aah divvint kna where they are noo, the must have been blaaing blidy miles away, ye've got te get help!'

Mike joined them, clinging onto them to stop him-self from being blown away and shouted, 'What's happened, where's the rest of the lads?'

Edward shook his head and said, 'Help me get Jake back to my car.'

It took the two of them five long minutes to help Jake back along the road and into the car, the wind making it tremendously difficult to hold the car door open while they got him inside. They then helped Jane from the Morris into the Jowett so that she could listen to Jake's story. It took Edward almost ten minutes to gather enough information from Jake's rambling take on events before he had an inkling of what had happened, 'So you didn't see the tent or the others being blown away?' he asked Jake who was huddled up on the front seat.

'Nur, tha had been blown away before I got back man, noo what are we ganna dee?'

Edward turned to Mike who was sitting in the back seat listening intently, 'I doubt they hev been blowing away, Aah reckon they must hev teken shelter somewhere, tha not daft; they wouldn't' stay outside in this.'

Jake interrupted him, speaking to him as though he was a child, 'Tha's nowhere te shelter there man, Aah've telt ye tha've been blaaing away, noo we need te get help!'

Leaning forward, Mike said, 'There is somewhere! I know where they'll be, tha's a pillbox not far from where they were camped, Aah bet they've taken shelter there.'

Jake hunched up even more and muttering, 'Ur aye, Aah'd forgotten aboot that,' and closed his eyes to rest.

Jane returned to the Morris and followed the Jowett as Mike guided Edward along the road and through the open gate onto the rough grass and path that led to the campsite. Climbing out of the car, Edward noticed that the wind had begun to drop and the rain had eased just a little as he walked back to the Morris to speak to Jane, 'Can you sit in my car and look after Jake while Mike and I go and search for the boys?'

Ian was sandwiched between Reg and Rafe for warmth as Howard finished stirring the stew he had just cooked on the ever faithful primus, 'Reet,' he said, We'll have te eat it straight oot the pot and we'll hev te share two spoons as that's all I cud find.'

The lads shuffled forward eagerly sniffing in the aroma of hot stewed steak as Mike crawled in out of the now rapidly dropping wind and said, 'It's alright, me and Mr Thompson have already eaten so we don't need any, I hope you lot are all okay?'

Seeing Edward join Mike in the confines of the doorway, Ian asked, 'What are ye two deeing here?'

'We've come to rescue you and take you home and just as well we did seeing as how your tent's gone, 'Mike replied.

Ian looked at the other lads and said, 'But we are okay, we'll spend the night in here and it sounds like the storms passing, we cannit leave wor bikes here noo can we?'

Edward added, 'You could leave your bikes in here and I'll drive ower in the van tomorrow and collect them.'

Rafe spoke up, 'Thanks for coming but I am sure I speak for all of us when I say, we'd rather spend the night here and ride back in the morning, besides we have to return the tarpaulin or what's left of it!'

'That's fine with me but after you've eaten I think you and Ian had better come over to the cars and say hello to Ian's mother, she drove through storm to get here and Jake is waiting in my car.'

Big Howard stopped shovelling stew into his mouth and asked, 'Jakes we you, hoo did that happen?'

Edward sniggered and replied, 'He was fleeing doon the road like a wind borne banshee and bumped inte me car, he's in a bit of a state!'

Fifteen minutes later, the wind had dropped to a breeze and the rain almost stopped with the sky beginning to lighten over the North Sea as the Hacky Dortys stood looking down at Jake huddled on the front seat of Edward's car, Ian asking, 'What happened Jake, ye look a right state?'

Jake looked up at them pathetically and replied, '*What happened, What happened*, I' tell ye what blidy happened, Aah got chased by ghosts and ghouls then I was captured by two great big nasty buggers who battered me heed and threw me oot inte the blidy storm,' he hesitated when he realised his pals were laughing at him, 'it's not funny man, then Aah got back te the camp and iviry thing had gone, Aah thowt ye's aall had been blaaing away so I ran te Seahooses te get help and Mr Blidy Thompson knocked me ower, Aah've had an aaful blidy night man!'

Still giggling, Ian said, 'Well we are staying in the pillbox tonight and biking hyem tomorrow, what are ye ganning te de?'

Jake opened the car door and replied, 'Stay we ye lot of course,' but Jane who had been talking to the boys, quietly and firmly pushed him back in and closed the door.

'You are going home young man, you have had quite enough adventure for one evening and there will be no arguing.'

The lads exchanged their sodden sleeping bags for the blankets that Mike had brought while Edward dropped the rear seat of Jane's little estate car and stowed Jake's bike inside. After telling the boys to be careful, Edward and Jane turned the cars and headed back to Ashington just as the dipping sun burst through the clouds behind the Cheviot way over to the west.

Having been dropped off by Jane, Jake propped his bike against the fence in the yard, and pulling his most pathetic of faces, let his shoulders sag and the still wet and stretched sleeves of his battered blue woollen jumper hang below his hands before shuffling into his house looking for sympathy!

Monty their scruffy black mongrel greeted him at the door with a couple of barks but when Jake tiredly pushed him away, he lost interest and returned to his blanket by the black-leaded kitchen range. Seeing that no one was in the Spartan kitchen cum living room, Jake walked to the sitting room door and looking in at his Mam, Dad and two younger brothers who were watching television, he adopted what he thought was the pose of a war weary soldier by raising his elbow up against the door frame and leaning to one side.

No-one turned to look at him so he said in a weary voice, 'Am back.'

No response - no-one turned to acknowledge him, their eyes firmly glued to the twelve inches of flickering television screen.

He took a deep breath and ranted, 'How man, am nearly deed from the storm, Aah've been chased by ghosts in Bamburgh Castle, smacked on the heed, hoyed oot inte the storm, soaked te the skin, battered and knocked doon by Mr Edward's car, am knackered, man – is tha oot te eat, am starving?'

Without turning, Flo Grundy snapped, 'Shut up man, Dixon of Dock Green's just finishing and we had wor tea hoors ago!'

'But am starving man!'

Albert Grundy eased forward in his arm chair and taking a handful of coins from his pocket, chose a shilling and again without turning, held it out for Jake, 'Here, gan te Polly's and get yersell pattie and chips.'

'Ur Dad man, am knackered, Billy will ye gan for me?'

Flo snapped, 'It's nearly ten a'clock, the bairn's not ganning oot noo, hadaway yersell and be blidy quiet man.'

Ten minutes later, Jake was sniffing up the wonderful aroma of fish and chips as he waited to be served in Polly's Fish and Chip shop in High Market. He was still damp and dishevelled with sand clinging to his clothes and his hair resembled an upturned bass broom but he didn't care the smell and sight of the golden chips drove away his fatigue.

Looking at Jake licking his lips, Polly said, 'Hello Jake lad, ye look in a right state, did ye get caught oot in the storm?'

'*Caught oot in the storm*! Aah nearly died in the storm man,' Jake replied ready to relate the horrors he suffered earlier but stopped when an auburn haired girl with a broad shy smile walked in and stood next to him waiting to be served. He recognised her as the lass who had moved into Ian's old house at the end of the Sixth Row and when he saw her smile, he changed his tune; straighten himself up, he pushed his dangling sleeves up his arms and pushing out his chest said without stopping for breath, 'Aah got trapped in Bamburgh Castle and chased a ghost and had te escape from two mad warders then Aah had te batta me way though the storm te where Aah was camping we me marras and Aah fund they'd all be blowing away so Aah had te run through the storm te Seahooses te get help and Aah got knocked ower but am alreet and Aah rescued me pals but noo am starving Aah've had nowt te eat since this morning - canna hev a meat pattie and chips please?'

With Julia Compton looking on admiringly, Polly replied, 'Eee, ye've had an aaful day Jake, I'll put in an extra pattie seeing that it's been quiet in here tonight because of the storm.'

Jake handed over his money and grabbing the open bag of food doused it in salt and vinegar before snatching a couple of very hot chips and stuffing them into his mouth but was then forced to go through facial gymnastics as he tried to stop the chips burning the inside of his mouth.

Giggling at Jake's facial expressions, Julia said to Polly, 'A mince pie and chips please, for me dad coming of night-shift.'

Despite his unkempt appearance, Jake tried to look nonchalant and said, 'Ye've just moved inte the end of wor street, in Ian's hoose hevn't ye, Aah'll waalk aroond hyem we ye as it's getting dark.'

Julia blushed and Polly said, 'By yor a canny lad Jake.'

Biting into the first Pattie, Jake spluttered through a mouthful of stodge, 'Aye that's me, Canny Jake, howeh then let's gan, what's yor name?'

'Julia,' she replied as she examined him thinking, 'he looks a right clip - but he has got a bonny face!'

Chapter Six
Homecoming

The long, uncomfortable and tedious train journey from Kuala Lumpur to Singapore in the rickety wooden carriage seemed never ending for Ronnie as he daydreamed of lying with his beautiful wife again. He purposely kept the killing of the Chinese terrorists out of his thoughts and tried to keep the problems of ensuring they were ready to travel to the UK next week at the back of his mind, being quite sure Mary would have everything organised for herself and the Army would ensure he was ready to travel!

Big Bill was thinking of the work left to be done before they departed on Monday, most of the preparation for the handover of the barracks had been completed before the Battalion had suddenly been whisked north along with all other available troops to oversee the surrender of the MNLA and capture or kill those that would not surrender before they escaped into Thailand. His company had gained enormous kudos from the killing of Lee Tan and Jay Jay the RSM had told him that the CO was writing Grundy up for a Mention in Dispatches. Bill smiled as he thought about the irrepressible Ashington Lad, thinking, 'He'll make a good SNCO - one day!'

Mary welcomed Ronnie home with all the enthusiasm he had hoped for and after two hours in bed, she dragged him downstairs for the meal she had prepared earlier, 'What happened in Malaya Ronnie, you see any bad Chinese this time?'

Standing behind her admiring her shapely figure in her loose fitting robe, he wrapped his arms around her and replied, 'We did this time Pet but it's all over now,' then kissing her neck he asked, 'are you ready to go?'

She turned in his arms and looking up at him, she smiled and answered, 'Of course Ronnie, I not stupid, I have had a few arguments with John but everything good now and he is having party for us tomorrow night, I'm booked on Britannia aeroplane on Tuesday so I arrive in England same day as you at Blackbushe.'

'That's what I hoped,' Ronnie said, 'we'll get the train to London and stay in the Union Jack Club before travelling up to Newcastle the following day.'

Mary broke away from his arms and said, 'Come, look I have a map of England and marked Blackbushe and Ashington, now you sure me where the Union Jack Club is and railway to Ashington.'

Ronnie swept her up in his arms and kissing her lightly said, 'Later Pet!'

By late Sunday afternoon, Bill had briefed, John Shelby, the new CSM on the personalities in the Company and wishing him well, said, 'I'll see you at Catterick and I expect the Company to be in good order when they arrive so ensure you keep them in check on the Troop Ship, Jay Jay will still be the RSM until the ship docks then the Battalion is mine including you and the Company.'

Smiling, Shelby replied, 'Aye Bill or should I say 'Sir', I've got the message, I'll look after your lads - well my lads now, and now if you don't mind Sir, you can leave me to get on with running the Company.'

After a very loud Chinese style party in the Lion Bar on Saturday night, Ronnie spent most of Sunday in camp being briefed on the flight home and the barracks and married quarters in Catterick. After the briefings the soldiers then completed relevant documentation including travel warrants for train journeys in the UK.

Big Bill warning them, 'After your disembarkation leave, I expect to see you all at Haig Barracks by twelve hundred hours on the twenty second of September and woe betide anyone who is late!'

The following morning, after a lingering kiss, Mary waved him off saying, 'Have a safe journey my Ronnie, see you in England on Friday!'

Back in Ashington; after Albert had gone to work and the bairns were outside playing, Flo Grundy picked up the blue air mail letter the Postman had dropped through the hardly ever used letter box and carried it carefully back into the kitchen and placing it on the table, she made herself a cup of tea. She recognised Ronnie's hand writing and seeing as it was the only letter he had written since returning to Germany after his leave at Christmas nine months past, she wanted to savour reading it. The letter was typical of Ronnie's short and to the point:

Hello Mam, Dad, Jake, Billy, Roger and Monty,

I hope this letter finds you all well, as I am as I write it. I will be home on Saturday the 6th of September when I have a couple of surprises for you. I have had a smashing time out here, looking forward to seeing you all and having some of Cuthbertson's fish and chips.

Ronnie.

Having read the short letter through a couple of times, Flo placed it on the table in front of her and lit a cigarette, saying out loud, 'Well that was hardly worth the bloody effort lad!' Only slightly built and with a well-worn, stern face and mannerisms to match that hid her kind heart, she was delighted with the letter and wondered what his surprises were.

'His National Service must be ower now so that cannit be one of the surprises,' she thought to herself, 'he's probably got some German lass pregnant, knaaing him!'

A couple of hundred yards away, against a backdrop of the sprawling colliery buildings and gigantic pit heaps, the Hack Dortys walked across the newly opened 'New Rec Bridge' that spanned the numerous railway lines of the colliery shunting yard behind the Sixth Row. They were discussing the differences between the old and new bridges, 'Whey this forst part isn't closed in like the owld one,' Jake said as he leaned over rail of the first section of the bridge.

Looking up at the slender concrete ladder like structure balanced on the five triangular shaped supports, Rafe said, 'I think this first length is very elegant whereas the second length is rather boring, it's just a concrete sided walkway but this part well look how tall and slender these concrete supports are.'

'They're a canny height like,' Ian added, 'they must be twenty foot high and that's on top of the walk way which is twenty foot high!'

'Too blidy high to jump off the top of them,' Jake said as he spat over the rail into a wagon full of coal below, 'but this bit is not much higher than the owld bridge, I reckon ye can still jump into the wagons.'

Howard glared at Jake and said, 'Look Jake what we want te kna is hoo are ye ganning te pay back the thirty bob it cost us when ye bornt the tent doon?'

Indignant, Jake replied petulantly, 'Howeh man lads it was an accident and Aah nearly bornt te death man, and Aah did run for help when Aah thowt ye were aall blaaing away noo didn't Aah?'

Despite his huge grin, Reg snapped back angrily, 'Aye and what aboot the blidy pies ye ate, ye greedy sod?'

'Look man Aah hevn't got thirty bob noo hev Aah and Aah ownly mek a pund a week on the paper roonds so ye'll hev te wait!'

'Whey am not happy aboot that,' snarled Howard, 'am ganning te throw the little waster ower the bridge', and reached for Jake who side-stepped his grab and ran off along the bridge and down the steps into the Miner's Recreational Grounds or 'Rec'.

Ian said, Let him gan Howard, he is starting te try to sort himself oot, he's taking ower my grocery delivery job next week and did you notice, he's combed his hair?'

'That's because he fancies that lass that moved into your owld hoose,' Howard said smiling, 'He'll be lucky eh?'

Rafe put his arm around Howard and said, 'Well you know Howard, below his ragamuffin looks, Jake is a good looking boy, *when* he has a wash and combs his hair!'

'Whey that's not very often is it?'

Their attention was drawn to the scream of a jet aeroplane over head, 'Wow look, a Hawker Hunter,' Reg said excitedly.

Watching the jet fly low and fast northward, Rafe asked, 'Where's that from?'

'RAF Acklington,' Ian replied, 'they have Hunters and Meteors and the air show is the weekend after next, hoo fancies ganning?'

'Aah think we'll all shud gan, even that scruffy git Grundy,' said Howard.

'That sounds great,' Rafe said, 'but how far is it and how do we get there?'

Pointing to the north-east, Ian said, 'On our bikes, it's a few miles away, just past Broomhill.'

Howard changed the subject and asked, 'Are ye two brain-boxes ready to start grammar school on Wednesday?'

Nodding, Ian replied, 'Aye, me Mam managed to change Rafe from Morpeth to Bedlington Grammar so we can travel together and wor uniforms will be the same. That reminds me, we've got te tell Jake to come and collect all of Rafe's old school clothes cos they're nee gud te us noo.'

Smiling at Ian, Rafe said, 'You didn't mention that a certain Peggy Reagan will be catching the same bus as us Ian, or had you forgotten?'

'Hardly; howeh let's find Jake.'

For the umpteenth time, without realising she was doing it, Jane looked out of the front window of Kirkup's Bakery, searching for any sign of the McArdles. Relieved not to have seen them, she was beginning to believe that the two thugs had given up harassing her for the money Nick owed them from their bet on the winner of the Grand National.

She was unaware that the McArdles had no intentions of giving up chasing the money they believed *she* now owed them; they had been very busy selling smuggled booze and fags to some of the less salubrious pubs and hotels in and around Blyth. Having being pressed for payment by the Ship's Officer who had supplied the contraband, the McArdles had felt it necessary to teach him not to push them and had roughed him up a little when they reluctantly handed over some of the money they owed him.

Back in their squalid caravan, Joe poured them both a whisky and said, 'Another couple of days will see most of the boxes gone, then Pat me lad I tink it will be time to put the pressure on the wida Shepherd, I tink with a bit of encouragement, she'll cough up a grand just to get us off her back!'

Joe grinned wickedly, adding, 'I'd settle for five hundred and a bit of action with the bonny Jane, she's got a lovely little arse on her,'

Pat took a slurp of his whisky and licking his lips, said, 'Now that's an idea Pat, we'll have to see if we can have some of that,' and laughed wickedly.

Having endured so much together over the years, John Peng bade his sister Mary a tearful farewell and the two of them promised to stay in touch as she walked off into the departure lounge of the airport, ready to face a new future with the man who had stolen her heart with his honest, open and unassuming but confident manner when he had courted her. She was leaving Singapore for the first time and although Ronnie had described it to her in great detail, she wondered what she would think of England and especially Ashington and worried as to how his parents would react when they found out their eldest son had married a Chinese girl! She was taking with her a complete new wardrobe of western style clothes copied from vogue magazines but made at a fraction of their original prices in the tailors' shops of Nee Soon, hoping they would help her blend in with the crowd, totally unaware that her stunning exotic looks and very fashionable new clothes would do exactly the opposite.

Back in the Sixth Row, Flo Grundy said, 'Eee my God, is that really ye Jake, ye look just like one of them posh lads,' as she admired her very self-conscious son who was trying his best to comb his hair into some semblance of order. Having arrived back from his paper round ten minutes previously, he had quickly donned the grey flannels, shirt and the tie that Ian had pre-tied for him to slip over his head and around his collar so that all Jake just had to do was tighten it.

Satisfied that he had tamed his hair, he took the dark purple school blazer that Rafe had worn at Rugley Public School and ceremoniously pulled it on before turning to look at his admiring mother, asking, 'Div a look a soft shite Mam?'

Flo took a long drag from her woodbine and after slowly blowing it out, she said smiling, 'Ye look like a million dollars bonny lad, noo divvint he dare get them mucky ora'll give ye a reet yarking!'

'Aye alreet Mam,' he replied as he left the house to hover by the front gate just as Howard strolled down the street.

'Ye can sod off Jake, yer not walking te school we me dressed like that,' Howard growled and walked on.

Jake didn't care, he hadn't been waiting for Howard; he stepped out of the yard as Julia Compton walked briskly toward him. Licking his hand, he pressed down the tuft of hair that kept springing up at the back of his head and said as she approached, 'Aah thowt Aah'd waalk around te school with ye te show ye where everything is like!'

Astounded at his appearance, she stopped and took a long look at the now very dapper Jake, could this really be the scruffy lad she had walked back from the fish and chip shop with, the one who had talked non-stop?

She was impressed but said, 'Aah've already been te the school, me Mam took me yesterday to speak te the teachers so Aah know how te get there.'

Looking down at his new-second-hand shoes, Jake said dejectedly, 'Oh.'

Seeing his crestfallen face, she said cheerfully, 'Come on then, we can still walk together can't we?'

Having acknowledged, Peggy Reagan, the pretty girl from the Sixth Row who, according to her, was his official girlfriend, Ian climbed onto the bus with her and Rafe for the journey to Morpeth Grammar and their first day there. They had a brilliant day, both lads making friends instantly, especially Rafe as the local lads were keen to find out all about Rugley School.

Jake's day started well enough but was somewhat spoiled when he walked into the boy's yard and was immediately confronted by Geordie Robertson; the school bully that Ian had defeated in along and vicious fight before the summer holidays.

'For fuck's sake look at this - Grundy all dressed up in somebody else's clothes cos he's got nowt of his an,' the bully sneered.

Remembering his Mam's warning not to mucky his new uniform, Jake turned away, trying to ignore Geordie but the bigger lad grabbed his arm and snarled, 'Divvint torn yer back on me ye little shite; Ian and his poncy uncle aren't here to protect ye noo!'

Realising he was in deep trouble, Jake turned ready to defend himself but Howard stepped forward, his meaty hand grabbing Geordie's as he warned, 'Nur tha not Geordie but Aah am and if ye divvint want another blidy hiding, Aah would bugger off and keep me gob shut if Aah was ye.'

His bravado gone, Geordie tried to pull his hand away but Howard held onto it for a few seconds to emphasise his warning before releasing it, allowing the chastised coward to slink a way, muttering obscenities.

Jake smiled at Howard and said, 'Ta but Aah wud hev fettled the pig mesell ye kna!'

Grinning at Jake, Howard replied, 'Aye of course ye wud Jake lad; hey we Hacky Dortys stick together; noo piss off ye ponce, yer embarrassing me dressed like that!'

Walking past the Holy Sepulchre Church on the way to spend lunch with her Mam; Jane's only daughter Maureen felt her baby kick, 'He's going to be a footballer this one,' she thought as she stopped to touch the spot where she had felt the baby.

A lovely September morning, she had never felt so alive and happy; she loved her new home in Wansbeck Road, especially now that her seventeen year-old husband Terry and his Dad had finished decorating. Just a few months ago she had been in the depths of despair; pregnant and afraid that her boyfriend would disown her when he found out, she felt unable to tell her Mam as her despicable Father had gone completely of the rails. Drunk most of the time he had lashed out at all of them making their lives' a living nightmare. Now newly married and in her own home thanks' to her Mam's inheritance and with her father out of their lives for good and her baby due in just over three weeks' time, she was happy and content.

Two swarthy and flashily dressed men standing outside the White House leered at her as she walked past them, one of them doffed his hat and said, 'Who's been a busy little girly then?'

A shiver of revulsion ran down Maureen's back as she hurried on and into Hotspur House where Jane was slicing tomatoes to go with the salad she was making, 'Hello Maureen Darling,' Jane said, 'Sit down and I'll pour you a cup of tea, how's my granddaughter this morning?'

Thoughts of the two men gone, Maureen replied, 'I think it is a grandson Mam, it feels as if he's been playing football in my belly all morning!'

The McArdles appeared to have gone when a little later, Jane kissed Maureen 'Cheerio' before she walked back to work and Maureen strolled slowly home. She did not see the twins step out of the doorway of the Whitehouse and follow her at a distance through the plantation, past Wansbeck School to her house in the Terrace facing the Park. Noting the number of the house, the two men turned around and whistling cheerfully, walked back toward the Portland Hotel where they had parked their old car and drove off to the Grand to try and catch a few punters for their under the table gambling.

In number 50 the Sixth Row, the first house in the last terrace and four doors down from the Grundy's, Irene Turnbull sat by the sitting room fire breast feeding six month old Rosalind as two year-old Raymond slept on the sofa and four year old Robert chased Max their Border Collie around the kitchen. Irene loved her children more than life itself and at thirty three was pleased with the tally so far, in addition to the three at home, she had five year-old Elizabeth, seven year-old John and nine year old Patricia, all of them at Wansbeck School and a very grown up eleven year old George at Bothal school. 'Another couple of months and I'll coax Geordie into having one more,' she thought, 'that will be enough then, the same as me Mam!'

Geordie, was typical of the hardworking miners that spent their working day toiling underground uncomplaining and pleased that since Nationalisation, work was constant and conditions improving. Now a Deputy responsible for one of the numerous coal faces in Ashington Colliery, he looked forward to eventually making Overman and going onto a salary. He needed to with so many mouths to feed and his Missus giving him that look again – well she always said she wanted eight bairns and he was happy to oblige as he loved the bairns as much as she did.

Irene sat baby Rosalind up and gently rubbed her back, helping the baby burp up the excess wind she had swallowed, then looking at the clock on the mantle, thought, 'Aggie will be here shortly for her afternoon visit!'

Forty eight year-old, five foot nowt Aggie Galloway or the 'Gallowa,' the mother hen of the street, bustled up and down visiting and helping those that wanted her, she would do anything for anybody and above all else, she loved bairns! Despite years of trying, she had never conceived and had never felt the need for either herself or husband Arthur to visit the Doctors to see if there was a problem in that department with either of them; besides there were plenty of bairns in the street to fuss over. Her favourite family was her old next door neighbours, Jane and her children. Aggie had always been there for them, especially during the dark years and now that they lived in High Market, she had become adept at finding reasons to call in; normally around tea-time!

    Late on Friday afternoon, Ronnie paced nervously back and forth in the arrivals lounge of Blackbushe airport, desperate to get through customs and baggage to see if Mary was waiting for him.

    Big Bill stepped in front of him and said, 'For God's sake Grundy lad, sit down and relax, she'll be there lad, yer tiring us out just watching you.'

    Ronnie sat down but his right heel began to rise and fall rapidly, bouncing his leg nervously as he replied, 'Am worried that she might be lost or the planes late or sumat Sir!'

    Shaking his head and smiling, Bill said, 'Look lad from what I've heard of your lass, she's more than capable of looking after herself and probably a darn sight better at it than you, now relax.'

    Big Bill was right; Mary was waiting with her two suitcases when Ronnie finally hurried through the customs and took her in his arms and kissed her gently before she hurried him along to a taxi to take them to the train station. On the train to London, she held his hand tightly as she looked out of the carriage window and pointed at buildings, asking Ronnie what they were. Unaware of what most of them were, he guessed as he sat smiling at her, enjoying her excitement.

    She was impressed with the faded Edwardian splendour of the Union Jack Club but not impressed at having to leave the room to visit the bathroom but her excitement was rekindled the following morning on the taxi ride through a grimy overcast London to Kings Cross to catch the 'Flying Scotsman' to Newcastle.

Big Bill was on the platform talking to Major Timison, the Battalion Second in Command who was in charge of the Advance Party. Seeing Ronnie and Mary loading their suitcases into a carriage, Bill walked up and said, 'See Grundy, I told you she would be waiting.'

Looking up at the huge Sergeant Major, Ronnie replied, 'Ye did Sir,' then coughing, he said very formally, 'Sir, this is my wife Mary!'

Bill took her tiny hand gently in his and looking down at the beautiful Mary dressed in a very smart pale blue jacket and skirt, he said, 'Pleased to meet you Mrs Grundy, you are as bonny as your husband's boasts, I hope you have a safe journey North and I will see you both in a fortnight.'

Ronnie asked, 'Are you not coming on the train Sir?'

Grinning, Bill replied, 'No lad, I'm picking up my new car in an hour and will be driving up home this afternoon, now go on get aboard.'

Later that afternoon as Bill drove North up the A1 in his new British racing green, Triumph TR3 sports car, Albert Grundy cursed as his spanner slipped of the spark plug of the Ariel motorbike he was tinkering with outside the air-raid shelter cum work shed opposite his house in the Sixth Row. Despite Flo telling him to keep clean as Ronnie was due home that day, Albert with fag dangling from his bottom lip was wearing his patched and very greasy navy blue overalls and equally battered and greasy flat cap as he struggled to free the over-tightened spark plug.

He was on his knees with his back to the road when just after four o'clock, the taxi carrying Ronnie and Mary from Ashington railway station pulled up behind him. Climbing out of the Taxi, they walked up behind Albert as the driver unloaded their suitcases.

Without turning Albert said over his shoulder, 'Is that you Ronnie lad?'

Mary held her finger to her lips to shush Ronnie and patting her hair unnecessarily, said, 'Hello Mr Grundy, I am Mary your daughter-in-law!'

Taken aback, Albert shuffled round on his knees and looking up at the beautiful and elegantly dressed Chinese girl, spluttered, 'Niva in the creation of cra's shite!'

Not understanding a word he had said, Mary frowned and said, 'I'm sorry Mr Grundy, I no understand you?'

Smartly dressed in grey slacks, blazer, white shirt and tie, Ronnie stepped forward to speak but Albert replied, 'Am sorry bonny lass but hoo on earth has wor Ronnie managed to marry Royalty like ye and what was a lovely China lass like ye deeing in Gurmany?'

Watching his father scramble to his feet, Ronnie said, 'Mary's from Singapore Dad, that's one of the surprises Aah hev for you.'

Albert stood gawping at Mary as she reached up; placing her hands on his greasy overalls and kissed him on the cheek.

'Eee be careful Pet,' Albert stuttered, 'Am aall greasy.'

Standing between her Husband and Father-in-Law waiting for the taxi to drive off, Mary looked at the row of low roofed houses and turned to look back at the row of toilets, coal houses and air-raid shelters opposite, then smiling at Ronnie said, 'You right my Ronnie, looks bad but feels like a nice place!'

Albert started excitedly across the road saying, 'Eeee wait till Aah tell yer Mam!'

'Nur hang on man Dad, Ronnie said, 'Let's hev a bit of fun, we'll let Mary gan in forst but Aah thought me Mam wud have seen us pull up?'

'She'll be watching tele with the two young'uns man,' Albert said as a voice boomed from down the Row.

'Ronnie! Ronnie,' Jake shouted from where he was playing football with Howard.

Ronnie waved at his younger brother, who, football forgotten, sprinted down the Row and screeched to a halt smiling gormlessly, 'Hello Ronnie, am glad yer back, is that ye finished in the army noo,' then turning to look at Mary, he blushed scarlet when he saw her smiling at him and said quickly, 'hello Missus, who are ye like? Are ye with wor Ronnie?'

Mary barely understood one word the breathless Jake had blurted and said, 'You must be Jake, I am very pleased to meet you, you look like a young Ronnie, I am Ronnie's wife,' and much to Jake's embarrassment, she leant forward and kissed him on the cheek.

Self-consciously, touching his cheek, Jake looked at Mary then Ronnie before asking, 'Is she really yor wife, cos she looks like a Chinky and right posh and bonny like?'

Ronnie ruffled Jake's hair roughly and said, 'Yes Jake she is my wife and she is Chinese, she is beautiful isn't she, now we better see Mam.'

Mary turned to her husband and said, 'Ronnie, I so glad we talked a lot so I get used to your funny language or I not understand anything here,' and raising her gloved hand, giggled like a little girl and instantly captured the hearts of Albert and Jake.

Sitting on the sofa in the sitting room with Billy on her right, Roger at her feet and Monty lying in front of the fire, Flo Grundy chuckled as Bill and Ben the flower pot men danced for Little Weed on the television. Roger sniffed up his dew drop and pushed his glasses back when Monty suddenly leapt up and ran out into the kitchen barking.

Jumping up, Flo said, 'That will be wor Ronnie back, Billy get yer jacket on cos he'll be wanting Cuthbertson's fish and chips,' and she scuttled into the kitchen where she stopped in her tracks to stare at the beautiful Chinese girl who was patting a madly tail-wagging Monty.

For once in her life, Flo was speechless and just stared at the exotic young woman in front of her as she wondered why she was standing in her kitchen smiling at her.

Mary broke the silence, 'Hello Mrs Grundy, I am Mary, Ronnie's wife!'

Flo shook her head not fully comprehending what Mary had said and asked, 'Whaat did ye say Pet?

Walking in behind Mary, a beaming Ronnie said, 'She said, her name is Mary Mam and she's my wife, now close yor gob and say hello.'

Mary walked up to Flo and gave a little bow, 'I am so sorry if I give you a shock, but Ronnie wanted it to be a surprise.'

'Surprise!' Flo said, 'It's a blidy surprise alreet Pet, who on urth has wor Ronald Married a foreign film star like ye,'

Mary giggled, embarrassed at the compliment and said, 'I'm not film star Mrs Grundy, I run Bar and a Brothel before Ronnie Marry me!'

From behind Ronnie, Jake asked, 'What's a brothel Ronnie?'

Albert looked worried and lifting his cap scratched his head nervously while Billy and Roger stood in the doorway of the sitting room staring at Mary as their mother pulled out a kitchen chair, sat down and said, 'Eeee, whey bugga my eyes!'

'It's not what ye think Mam and Aah hev a couple more surprises for ye.'

'Nowt cud surprise me noo Bonny Lad,' and turning to a baffled Mary, she said, 'come on inte the sitting room and sit by the fire, you must be tired oot travelling aall the way from Gurmany?'

Mary followed Flo into the sitting room and said, 'We have not come from Germany Mrs Grundy, we have come from Singapore.'

When Mary sat down in the large old armchair next to the fire that burned unnecessarily on a warm September night, Flo asked, 'Singapore! Is that in China?'

Walking like conjoined twins, Billy and Roger stepped into the sitting room and stood directly in front of Mary gawping like idiots as Mary replied, 'No Mrs Grundy, Singapore is at the tip of Malaya.'

'Whey is Malaya in China then cos ye look Chinese te me Pet?'

Ronnie stepped in, 'No Mam, Malaya isn't in China but it's ower in that part of the world and Singapore has lots of Chinese living there, as well as Malayans and Indians.'

A totally confused Flo asked, 'But what wore ye deeing ower there when yer supposed te be in Gurmany man?'

I signed on for nine years and was posted there when my Battalion in Germany disbanded; we were in Malaya fighting...'

Flo stopped him with, 'Fighting, who the blidy hell hev ye been fighting noo? Aah hope ye hevn't got inte any trouble fighting?'

'No Mam man, we were fighting Chinese Terrorists up in Malaya.'

Still confused, Flo asked, 'Howay man, if ye wor fighting the Chinese, hoo come ye married one lad?'

'Mam, the ones we were fighting wor communist terrorists, Mary was not one of them man!'

Roger sniffed up his dew drop again and looking over the top of his glasses at a now bewildered Mary, said, 'She smells lovely, dee aall Chinky lasses smell like that Ronnie?'

Grabbing Roger by the arm, Albert marched him and Billy to the back of the sofa and told them to be quiet as Jake asked, 'Did ye kill any baddies then Ronnie?'

Without thinking and exasperated, Ronnie said, 'Aye man noo hang on while I explain everything.'

Flo's face was a picture as she digested this latest nugget before she said, 'Reet Ronald blidy Grundy, sit doon and tell me what the hell is ganning on!'

A reluctant Billy was dispatched to fetch fish and chips as Ronnie, sitting on the arm of Mary's chair, explained to his parents the events of the past nine months, Flo punctuating his story with 'Eeees' and 'Oooohs.'

It was Albert who summed it up, 'So lad, let's get this straight, ye didn't gan back te Gurmany after Christmas, ye flew oot te Singapore, ye've signed on for nine years and ye had a stripe but ye last it and noo ye've got it back and finally ye've married this bonny wee lassie who has had a helluva a time and ye've dragged hur from Singapore te Ashington, oh and ye've killed some terrorists, is that reet?'

'Aye Dad that's it – sort of anyway.'

From behind the sofa, Jake asked, 'Aye but hoo many baddies did ye kill man?'

Ronnie glared at him and replied, 'Just a couple noo divvint ask aboot that again.'

Flo rose from the sofa where she had sat speechless during Ronnie's story and standing in front of Mary said,' Eee Lass yer the bonniest Aah've iver seen and yer welcome inte this family even if ye are a Chinky, Aah mean Chinese and from noo on am yer Mam, alright Pet.'

Understanding most of what Flo had said, Mary replied, 'I am very happy to be here and I promise to make Ronnie a good wife, Mrs Grundy – Mam.'

When Billy returned from Cuthbertson's, Flo hurried into the kitchen and snatched the condiment set from the kitchen table and placing them on the dropped flap of the new kitchen blue and cream dresser standing by the pantry door, she pointed to the open oven door of the huge black-leaded range and said, 'Billy put the fish and chips there while Aah set the table.

Billy placed the huge bag of fish and chips on the door of the oven then turned to look at his Mam, who having wiped the bare table, was pulling apart an oiled table cloth that had been folded for so long that it had stuck together! Beginning to become flustered, she snapped, 'Billy, get the knives and forks oot the draw while Aah get some plates.'

Looking puzzled, Billy asked, 'What for Mam, we alwas eat wor fish and chips oot the paper man?'

'Not the neet, not we Ronnie's new wife here; noo get the knives and forks and Jake, get off yer arse and make a pot of tea, Albert ye ask the lass if she wants a bottle of stout.

Ronnie put his arm affectionately round Flo's shoulders and said, 'Calm doon Mam, it'll be nice for us all te sit at the table te eat and Mary doesn't drink but am sure she'd love a cup of tea.

Jane smoothed down her close fitting mauve ball gown as Doctor Metcalf pulled his Rover 90 smoothly to a halt outside Hotspur House in High Market. Sitting in the front passenger seat, his daughter Jennifer said, 'Have a lovely time tonight Dad and I'll be waiting for you to pick me up when you drop Mrs Trevelyan off,' and smiled as Mike who had been waiting for their arrival opened her door and took her hand to help her out of the car.

Mike said, 'Hello Jennifer, you are just in time for us to catch the bus down to the Arcade,' and kissed her on the cheek as Jonathon switched of the engine, looked into his rear view mirror to check that his bow tie was in place before climbing out and hurrying to the door of Jane's house.

Stepping back when she opened the door, he handed her a single rose and said, 'You look ravishing Jane dear,' and holding his arm up said, 'Shall we?'

They walked out to Jonathon's car as Edward drove by in his new Sunbeam Rapier that he had bought to take Jane to the Ball before discovering that he had been beaten to it by the Doctor.

'I think we are going to have a smashing night Edward,' Sandra, Edward's date for the Ball said as she placed her hand gently on his thigh.

Edward coughed nervously and looking at the glamorous divorcee, replied, 'Aah hope so Pet,' and removing her hand carefully said, 'Aah better concentrate on getting us there safely!'

Driving steadily North and not wanting to race the engine of his new car until it was 'run in', Bill Armstrong had thought about his son Wilhelm and ex-wife Irma. It had been four years since the divorce, four years since he had seen his son who was now aged ten. Stationed in Germany after the war, Bill had met Irma at a market in heavily bomb damaged Dortmund where she was selling clothes for food. Taken by her striking Germanic, blonde haired and blue eyed looks, he revisited the market three times before he finally picked up the courage to ask her for her date, which to his surprise, she readily accepted and they began seeing each other regularly.

When she fell pregnant and accepted Bill's proposal, he applied for permission to marry her and after a lengthy wait, they married a month before their son was born. It was much later that he came to realise that she had used him as a means of escaping her impoverished life in battle-scarred Germany. Initially it appeared as though the marriage was perfect but Irma soon began to demand more and more, making it clear that she had been used to a privileged life before the war. When Bill's unit moved back to the UK in 1950 and knowing that her parents were once more making money, she refused to go and moved back in with them as their engineering business began to boom after several very difficult post war years.

Irma made it clear that she would not leave Germany and that their son would be educated there, going out of her way to ensure Bill saw very little of either of them. Realising he had been used and that she had never had any real love for him, Bill made enquiries to see if he could gain custody of Wilhelm but his efforts were cut short when the Battalion shipped out to join the Commonwealth Brigade fighting the war in Korea. On his return and with a Military Medal added to his collection, he came to terms with having been divorced and having lost visiting rights with his son thanks to the German Courts interpretation of Irma's take on events.

Pulling up outside his mother's Victorian terraced house in North Seaton Road in Newbiggin just before eight o'clock, he decided he would visit his son one more time in an effort to re-establish his role as the boy's father.

Both his Mother and Aunt were waiting to greet him when he breezed in and he hugged them both before saying, 'It's good to be home for a bit Mam, you are both looking champion, now I'd murder a cup of tea and talking of murder, I want to hear what the blidy hell happened to our Nick!'

Margaret Shepherd, Bill's Aunt and mother of the convicted and hanged police murderer, Jane's husband Nick Shepherd, said, 'Bill it's a very upsetting story and probably best left until tomorrow when yer rested from ye lang journey.'

Nodding, Bill said, 'Aye yer probably right Aunty Margaret but I want te get te the bottom of it and want to know what part these so-called gangsters, the McArdles had te play in it.'

His Mother poured him a cup of tea before walking to the sideboard in the corner of the old-fashioned sitting room to pour a whisky for her son and a glass of sherry each for herself and her sister. Handing the drinks to the other two she said, 'First a toast to the safe return of me big bonny son, welcome home Bill.'

Knocking back the whisky, Bill said, 'Thanks Mam and Aunty Margaret, it feels as though Aah've never been away.'

Sitting down next to her sister, his mother said, 'Me and yer Aunty Margaret will tell ye all we can in the morning but Aah think ye better call in and see Jane and talk to her to find oot what was going on, suffice te say, Nick wasn't the man ye thowt he was!'

Bill nodded, 'Aah know he was no saint Mam, but killing a policeman, that teks some believing!'

After parking outside the mighty Alnwick Castle, Edward and Sandra walked through the imposing double gated entrance into the castle grounds, dominated by the massive central building, the home of the Dukes of Northumberland. A gentle September breeze fluttered the flames of the burning torches that lined the coconut matting laid across the lawn to a huge marquee where they could hear a band playing a quick step. Looking very fetching in a low cut blue ball gown, Sandra was obviously excited and clung to Edward's arm as they joined the small queue to hand in their invitations and at the entrance to the marquee before being shown to their seats.

'Hello Edward, I didn't know you were coming,' Jonathon Metcalf said as he and Jane walked up behind them.

Edward turned and replied, 'Why would you? Can I introduce you to Sandra Phillips, an old friend?'

Sandra tutted at Edward, then smiling said, 'Not so much of the 'old' please Eddie!'

She then took Jonathon's outstretched hand and held onto it with both of hers as he said, 'Hello Sandra – I'm Doctor Jonathon Metcalf; I believe I know your father.'

While Jonathon and Sandra discussed her father, Jane reached up and kissed Edward lightly on the cheek and said, 'I hope you find time for a dance with me tonight Edward.'

'So do I,' Edward replied as Sandra, seeing the look in Jane's eyes grabbed Edward's arm again and said, 'Come on Eddie darling, we are being shown to our table.'

The inside of the huge marquee was brightly lit with chandeliers and beautifully decorated with flowers, bunting and ribbons. Edward and Sandra joined a dozen others from Ashington Round Table at an apt circular table while Jonathon and Jane joined their group a couple of tables away. The evening started slowly with polite conversation but with the aid of drinks, good food and an excellent dance band, the marquee was soon filled with laughter and chatter and the dance floor full of elegant women in their ball gowns being whisked around by men in mainly black dinner suits, one or two in white jackets and two or three in military Mess Uniform.

Despite her slim figure, Sandra ate and drank with gusto and spent most of the remainder of the time on the dance floor with Edward or one of the other men at the table who were more than happy to oblige the vivacious blonde. Edward had looked over at Jane whenever he could to see if there was an opportunity to ask her to dance but Jonathon and the other men around her kept her fully occupied. It wasn't until after twelve o'clock when some of the revellers had left that the opportunity to dance with Jane presented its self!

A very merry Jonathon swaggered over to the Ashington table where he bowed to Sandra and said, 'Sandra, I cannot let the evening pass without just one dance with such a glamorous lady, would you care to join me?'

Slightly tipsy, Sandra giggled and held out her hand saying, 'I'd love to,' and the two of them walked off to the dance floor in animated conversation.

Seeing Jane sitting one her own, Edward walked quickly over and said, 'At last Jane lass, can we have that dance now?'

She smiled at him and pushing back the empty chair next to her, she replied, 'Not just yet Edward dear, can we just sit and talk for a while, I'm worn out!'

He sat down and he two of them chatted about the evening, when Maureen's baby was due and the boys until the band came to the end of the tune they were playing and Edward saw Jonathon and Sandra heading back, 'I still haven't danced with you yet Jane,' he said.

She leaned forward and kissed him lightly on the lips and said, 'I am sure we are going to have many dances together Edward just, perhaps not tonight.'

Sandra and Jonathon both saw the kiss and after escorting Sandra back to her table, Jonathon glared at Edward as he passed him on the way back to their chairs.

Sitting down next to Jane, he said tetchily, 'It looks as if you may have come with the wrong man this evening Jane!'

She smiled and replied, 'You did ask me first Jonathon.'

The Grundy's house had also been full of chatter and laughter for most of the evening as the family celebrated Ronnie's return and meeting his beautiful young wife. Ronnie had handed his father a bottle of Haig's whisky, his mother two hundred cigarettes, the two of them enjoying smoking and drinking the duty frees. Roger and Billy were given padded black jackets with garishly embroidered eagles on the back as Jake waited to see what his big brother had brought him.

'Here ye are Jake kidda,' Ronnie said as he handed him a black leather zip up jacket and a pair of American jeans, 'Aah thought ye might be owld enough to wear these noo, I've a couple of white Tee shirts te gan with them somewhere!'

Jake took the clothes almost reverentially from his brother and without saying anything nodded at him and walked quietly out of the sitting room and through the kitchen and disappeared upstairs.

Mary placed her hand on Ronnie's arm and asked, 'Is Jake alright Ronnie?'

Smiling wistfully, Ronnie replied, 'Yes Mary Pet, he's fine, that's exactly hoo Aah wud hev been if somebody had given me them when Aah was his age.'

Mary then handed two under-stated but exquisite silk blouses to Flo saying, 'For you Mam, I make them myself.'

Flo flung her cigarette-end into the fire and wiping her hands on her pinnie, gently picked one of the blouses up and said, 'Eeee, ye shudn't hev but eeeee aren't tha beautiful, Aah'll be frightened to wear these in case Aah spoil the buggas!'

Albert was equally taken aback when Mary handed him two handmade shirts and said gruffly, 'Ta Pet, tha was nee need te gan te all this bother noo!'

Mary said, 'It was my pleasure Mr Grundy, now I am very tired and would like to go to bed please, Ronnie can you show me where this Netty is you tell me about.'

Flo jumped up and scuttled into the pantry returning with a battered lantern which she handed to Ronnie, 'Hear lad light this and stand ootside the netty while Mary is in there,' and turning to Mary, she said, 'Am sorry we just hev the outside lavvy Pet but Aah dee keep it nipping clean!'

Trying to look serious, Mary said, 'That is no problem to me Mam, I have always had to use an outside toilet!'

A few minutes later as she undressed in Ronnie's cramped bedroom, Mary looked at the large single bed and said, 'We will be cosy in there Ronnie!'

Grinning, Ronnie said, 'Aye we will Pet, thank God me Mam's washed the sheets!'

Snuggling up together Mary said very seriously, 'Ronnie, I love your family but we cannot stay here.'

Worried that his parent's house wasn't good enough for his exotic wife, Ronnie said, 'Am sorry Mary love, Aah kna it's nowt like your house and we haven't got a bathroom but...'

Mary stopped him, 'No Ronnie, that's not the problem, we cannot be husband and wife in this bed with your family next to us, it Okay for one or two nights but not for a whole two weeks!'

'But we've nowhere else te gan Pet, Aah don't take over wor married quarter until the nineteenth.'

'Can we stay in a hotel or somewhere we can go to be private Ronnie?'

'Aah canna afford a hotel Pet.'

She snuggled even closer and said, 'Yes you can Ronnie.'

'Aah, cannit man, Aah need what money Aah have for wor leave.'

'Yes I know but you have dowry money!'

Leaning up, Ronnie looked down into Mary's beautiful eyes and asked, 'What dowry money?'

'I bring it with me, well some of it, we can use that, if you want.'

Ronnie thought for a moment and said, 'But the nearest Hotel that Aah kna of is in Morpeth, six miles away, we'll hev te get the bus back and forward all the time.'

Pulling Ronnie back down, Mary whispered, 'Maybe we need a car Ronnie, what do you think, how much is a nice car?'

He sat up, 'Mary a canny car will be a couple hundred of quid, hoo much money did you bring?'

'Just two thousand Ronnie.'

'Just two thousand – what pounds?'

'Well yes pounds, I didn't bring dollars, I thought you would want pounds!'

Thinking of the kiss he had seen Jane give Edward and wondering if he was a serious rival for Jane's hand and not wishing to spoil the evening by saying something spiteful, Jonathon said very little on the drive back to Ashington. He was disappointed that Jane just kissed him on the cheek and thanked him for a wonderful evening and after waking Jennifer up who had been asleep on the sofa, he drove home in a morose mood.

Edward had the opposite problem with a very amorous Sandra and after declining the offer of a night cap and gently taking her clinging arms from around his neck; he bade her goodnight and hurried back to his car and drove home thinking of Jane's kiss.

The following morning, a light drizzle carried on a gentle breeze from the east freshened Bill's face as he strode briskly along Newbiggin's curving promenade, heading toward Church Point and a walk across the moor. He had risen early and feeling the need to clear his head, quickly drank a cup of tea and devoured two slices of toast before heading out, just as his mother came downstairs.

He was looking forward to the challenges of being the Regimental Sergeant Major but first he wanted to get to the bottom of his cousin Nick's demise and the part the McArdles had in it and he had decided that next weekend he would to travel to Germany to see if he could see his son. He had not received a reply to the letter he had sent to Irma but he was still determined to try and be part of his Wilhelm's life.

Sitting down at the kitchen table with a cup of tea after his refreshing three mile walk, he looked at his Mother and Aunt who were nervously waiting. He smiled and said, 'You look as though you're waiting to have your teeth pulled, I just want to know the full story that's all, so Mam, what happened?'

It was his Aunt Margaret who told the story of Nick's alcohol fuelled decline, his mistreatment of Jane and their children, his under the table betting and his affair with Ginny.

He interrupted her and asked, 'But what about the McArdles, where do they fit in?'

Sighing, she said, 'They only appeared on the scene a couple of weeks before the Grand National and forced him to take their money for a big bet, he tried to refuse apparently but they made him take it, anyway; their horse won and Nick was terrified that they were going to take his car and his money and hurt him so he got blind drunk, went hyem te get some more money and found the Proudlocks there talking about the wedding of Maureen and their son Terry. Nick hadn't known she was pregnant and hit her; of course young Terry tried to stop him and that was when Nick stabbed him!'

'Good God,' Bill said, 'what happened to Terry, is he okay?'

'He's champion, he was in hospital for a few days but the cuts weren't serious and him and Maureen are married noo and the baby's due anytime.' Sighing deeply, she continued, 'So niver mind; Nick runs around te High Market to the floozy Ginny and grabs his bag of cash and runs doon stairs, straight inte the McArdles but before they can dee owt, the Polis turns up and Nick jumped inte his car and drove off with them chasing him. He was as drunk as owt and crashed his car at Bothal Bank and when one of the Polis opened his door, Nick stabbed the poor lad and him with a wife and canny bairns.'

'Bill asked, 'So was that when he was arrested?'

His mother took up the story, 'No Pet, Nick ran off toward Coneygarth and bugga my eyes but he bumps into his lad Ian and Rafe.'

'Who is Rafe?'

'Whey man he's Jane's younger brother, he's the same age as Ian and when Jane's father died, he went te live with Jane. Anyways, Nick threatened Rafe and cut his neck so his own bairn Ian, bashed him on the heed with a pit prop and they ran off.'

Margaret took over again, 'He hid behind the netty wall while everybody was searching for him and snuck inte his hoose later that night when ivery body was in bed but the Polis saw him and caught him thank goodness. Nick was taken away and he pleaded guilty to iviry thing so was hung on the fifth of May.'

Bill scratched his head, 'You don't seem to upset about them hanging your lad Aunty Margaret?'

'Eeee Bill if ye ownly knew all the wicked things he got up to or saw poor Jane after he battered her or the way them poor bairns were terrified of him, I had to leave after my poor Jim died and tha's another story there but enough said aboot that.

His mother added, 'Aye and the McArdles are noo chasing Jane for the money that Nick owed them, they are a couple of bad buggas, Aah think ye shud gan and speak to Jane and that other bugga Ginny and let them tell ye what they kna.'

Bill nodded, 'Aye I think I will Mam but it will have te wait until Tuesday, I have a few other things to do and people to see first, and I need to see about a ferry as I want to try and see my lad in Germany.'

Sitting huddled in front of the sitting room fire, Mary took the cup of tea Ronnie handed and said, 'Thank you Ronnie, it looks dull outside and a bit cold today.'

'Aye Mary love, there's a bit of drizzle and it is a bit colder, summer's coming to a close like.'

She grinned and asked, 'Will we have snow, I never seen snow?'

In the kitchen, Flo took the cigarette from her mouth and said, 'Wa boond te hev snow bonny lass, and am sure ye'll hev some doon in Catterick, that's another cowld blidy hole.'

Mary looked up at Ronnie and asked, 'Can we walk around Ashington today Ronnie, I like to have a look round?'

'Course we can but mind all the shops will be shut but a couple of the cafés will be open.'

Furiously combing his hair into what he thought was a quiff, Jake said from the Pantry, 'The Buff Café is normally open on a Sunda,' and turning the collar of his new leather jacket up he walked to the back door and out into the lane hoping his new look would impress anyone there but especially Julia. He was disappointed, the drizzle appeared to have kept everyone in doors and after 20 minutes he was wet and with his hair dropping down over his forehead, just as the drizzle stopped and the clouds began to break, he gave up and walked back into the house as Billy passed him on the way to the outside toilet.

Flo looked at her damp son as he took his wet leather jacket off, 'Hev ye been standing oot in that rain?'

'Aah was just looking te see if any of the lads wor oot,' he lied.

Shaking her head, Flo looked at him and muttered, 'Sacklass Sod!'

A few minutes later while Jake dried himself in front of the kitchen fire; Billy walked back in and said, 'How Jake your gorlfrend is outside.'

Flo looked at her son and smiling, asked, 'Hev ye got a lass wor Jake?'

Jake didn't answer; he just glared at Billy as he made for the door, grabbing his leather jacket from the back of a chair where he had hung it to dry. Outside he saw Julia walking down to the end of the Row and looking like a demented Charlie Chaplin, he walked quickly after her slowing as he reached her.

Flicking back his drooping hair and trying to be nonchalant, he asked, 'Hiya Julia, where are ye ganning?'

She stopped when she saw him and asked, 'Why are ye dressed like that Jake?'

Adjusting his jacket casually he replied, 'Why what's wrang with me new clathes like?'

'Nothing if you want to look like that Jake I suppose!'

Jake was dumfounded, he thought he looked cool just like the older lads he saw walking round town, the ones who had been Teddy Boys but were now switching to leather jackets and jeans and asked, 'Look like what?'

'Like a tearaway Jake, are ye a tearaway?'

He thought for a moment before replying, 'No Aah divvint think see like, but this is what aall the lads are wearing noo man!'

'So ye want te look like everybody else then?'

'Aye, why not dee ye not think it's gud like?'

Julia smiled at him and said, 'It does a bit Jake, noo are ye coming with me to Chapel or are ye just out for a walk.'

He hadn't for a moment thought that she might be going to the Chapel and without thinking blurted, 'Aye am ganning te the Chapel, Aah often gan on a Sunday like!'

An hour later, the sun had chased away the clouds, as Ronnie led Mary through the cuts between the Colliery Rows, pointing out his old school – Bothal as they walked past it and onto the main road leading to High Market.

As they approached Gibson's, Ronnie said, 'We should have a look in the window of their new showroom, they might have a nice car in there!'

There were three cars in the showroom, a new grey Morris Oxford and a new green Wosleley 4/90 both of which were more than Ronnie wanted to pay but it was the other car that grabbed both of their attentions – a pre-owned red Riley one point five – Nick's car!

After the police chase and crash, Gibson's had recovered the car and repaired the damage that consisted of replacing the front bumper and right hand wing and lamps. With the outstanding hire purchase to be cleared and the repairs to be taken into account, they offered Jane fifty pounds for the car which she was glad to accept, not wanting anything to do with her dead husband's car.

Mary said, 'A red car Ronnie, red is colour for good fortune, joy and luck for Chinese, can we buy that one?'

Smiling he replied, 'Aah think it is great, it's a lovely looking car and it's ownly two hundred so yes Aah think we should buy that one, once I've had a look over it and checked it out the morn when they are open now come on Aah'll show ye Ashington.'

Chapter Seven
Good Riddance

The following day, having viewed the car and arranged the paperwork including insurance, Ronnie and Mary took delivery of the freshly polished Riley on Wednesday morning and went for a spin to Newbiggin, parking outside Bertorelli's Rivera Café overlooking the curving promenade. After a cup of frothy coffee they walked arm in arm along the promenade that was very quiet on an overcast working-day morning, Mary remarking, 'It is very peaceful here Ronnie and I like the sea.'

'It is nice here Mary Pet, how about staying here for the rest of wor leave, we can book into the 'Old Ship' and watch the fishermen setting oot in tha cobles.'

Mary was delighted with his suggestion and asked, 'What is a coble?'

Pointing to several gaily painted, open fishing boats lined up on the beach next to the small square that separated the Rivera Café from the Old Ship Hotel, he replied, 'Them pet, tha bonny boats aren't they?'

Mary nodded happily as they strode back to the hotel to book in.

Heading back to the Sixth Row at twelve o'clock to collect their belongings, Ronnie parked outside Billy Scott's shop and Post Office in High Market.

Switching off the engine, he said, 'Aah'll just be couple of minutes Mary, I am going to get my Post Office Savings Book brought up to date,' then climbed out of the car and walked round and disappeared into the shop just as two swarthy men in suits and fedoras approached the Riley.

Pat McArdle walked round to the front of the car and stared in at Mary, 'Would you look at this Joe, there's a Chinese Tart sitting in our car, now what the hell do you think she's doing in there?'

Standing next to the passenger door, Joe McArdle smiled down at Mary and circled his hand to indicate he wanted her to wind her window down.

Mary did so and smiling nervously at the heavily built man, asked, 'Yes, what do you want please,'

'I'll tell you what I want darling,' Joe sneered, 'I want you to tell me what you are doing in me and my brother's car?'

Confused and just a little afraid, Mary replied, 'This is not your car, my husband buy it on Monday, it is our car!'

Pat joined his brother at the side of the car and said, 'Now there you have a problem girlie, you see me and Joe have an old wreck of a car and we want this one cos it should be ours, we were going to buy it so you've made a mistake unless you would like to spend some time with us to change our minds.'

Mary began winding the window up but Joe lent on it with his arm and snarled, 'Now don't be rude darling, that's not nice.'

Walking out of the shop, Ronnie saw the McArdles leering in at Mary and snarled, 'What's ganning on here, who the hell are ye two?'

Turning to look at Ronnie, Joe said sarcastically, 'We're just asking yer little Chinese bint what she's doing in our car lad but now that you're here, you can tell us.'

'It's not your blidy car, it's mine I've just bought it now bugga off,' Ronnie growled as he started to walk past the brothers.

Pat stepped in front of him, 'Look Laddie, me and my brother want this car, it's owed to us by that waster Nick Shepherd, so you need to think about giving it to us for a few quid or something nasty might just happen to you or your tart!'

Struggling to control his anger, Ronnie snapped, 'You two must be the blidy McArdles, me Dad towld me about ye two last night and how the men in the Sixth Ra chased ye oot the street, whey ye divvint scare me and ye can bugga off the pair of ye.'

Mary said worriedly, 'Please Ronnie, get into car and we leave now.'

But both McArdles had stepped in front of him, Joe twiddling his silver dollar between his fingers, said, 'I think ye need to be very scared Laddie, me and Pat here want that car and we'll give ye fifty quid for it and a night with yer tart or ye might just have a nasty wee accident!'

Ronnie stepped back and with a cold glint in his eyes, said calmly, 'That is my wife you are talking about and I warn you two now, you have no idea who you are talking to, I will come after the pair of ye and get rid of ye one by one like the rats ye are if ye bother me or my wife again so tek my advice and get oot my way.'

Joe gave a mocking laugh and snarled, 'You don't scare us Laddie,' and snapped his teeth at Ronnie but moved back a little. Without taking his eyes of the two men, Ronnie walked around the car and climbed in, pausing to control his trembling hand before starting the engine and driving slowly away as the McArdles turned and walked back toward the White House club.

Bill had been very busy and had only just found time to drive over to Ashington to visit Jane; having telephoned her in the morning and arranged to call in at lunch time, he parked outside Hotspur House just after twelve. Climbing out of his car he straightened his tie, fastened his tweed jacket and walked around to the pavement just as the McArdles approached, both of them slowing as they watched the big man going up to Jane's door. Not wanting to be seen just yet, the brothers hurried past and headed to the end of High Market, past the White House Club, into the plantation on past the church and into Wansbeck Road.

Opening the door, Jane looked at up at Bill; it was years since she had last seen him and she had forgotten how tall and powerfully built he was.

As tall as Edward he must be a good stone or more heavier, she thought as she said, 'Hello Bill, it is lovely to see you looking so tanned and fit even if it is under awkward circumstances.'

Bill smiled and said, 'Lovely to see you again Jane lass and yer as bonny as I remember ye, am sorry if all this upsetting you but I just want to get to the bottom of what happened because despite all his faults, Nick was always good te me and he was a decorated hero.'

Jane shook her head as she led Bill into the sitting room, 'I'm sorry Bill but he was never a hero, all of that was brought out into the open during his trial.'

Looking perplexed, Bill asked, 'What are you saying, that he didn't win the MM?'

'That's correct Bill, Edward Thomson was the one that knocked the German machine gun out not Nick, Edward was wounded in the head and lost his memory for a few months and never said anything about it when he did remember, after all they had been friends once.'

Bill nodded, 'I remember Edward; he is a good man, someone you can rely on.'

He noted a little smile on Jane's face when she said, 'Yes he is.'

'So Jane is it true that Nick beat you and the kids?'

Taking in a sharp intake of breath, Jane composed herself before telling Bill of her terrible life with Nick and of how this year, it had become unbearable as he drank more and more and spent more and more time with Ginny. She then described the affect the McArdles had upon him and how they had been pestering her and how afraid of them she was.

Bill asked, 'And the McArdles are now bothering you for the money that Nick owed them, is that right?'

'Yes Bill, they say I have to pay them five hundred pounds or they will cause trouble or hurt me, they do scare me and I'm thinking that I should pay the money just to get rid of them.'

Something clicked with Bill, 'Are the McArdles about five feet eight, heavily built and look like gypsies?'

'That's them and they always wear hats not caps, why have you seen them?'

'I think I might have seen them earlier,' then not wishing to alarm Jane, 'I think I drove past them down town. I don't think you should pay them Jane, they will only ask for more if you do, I think you should have the police deal with them.' Standing up he continued, 'Look Jane thanks for talking to me and again I'm sorry if has been upsetting but I think I have a better idea of what happened now, if it is alright, I will leave my car outside and walk down to the Fell-em-Doon and speak to this Ginny to see what she has to say and I would like to speak to the McArdles as well and I will do if I see them around and about. Hopefully the next time we meet up we won't have to talk about such unpleasant matters.'

Jane nodded and at the door shook his massive outstretched hand as he left and headed off to speak to Ginny.

Maureen was sitting knitting or trying to knit; ever since her mother-in-law Sarah had shown her how to knit she had been trying to get to grips with it as she prepared for the birth of her baby in two weeks' time. Concentrating on not dropping a stitch as she struggled with a particularly intricate section, she was annoyed when a loud knock on the front door distracted her. Carefully placing the knitting to one side, she eased herself forward and holding her huge bulge, heaved herself slowly to her feet and walked to the door shouting, 'Just a minute!' as the another louder knock rattled the door.

Opening the door she stepped back in shock as the two burly men who had spoken to her last week pushed forward, one of them standing in the hall, preventing her from closing the door leered at her and said, 'Now then girly, me and my brother, don't want to upset you but we're wanting you to have a word wit your Mammy.'

Maureen tried hopelessly to push him back out of the hall but he grabbed her hand and leaning into her face, he snarled, 'Look lovey, you tell your Mammy that the McArdles want their money now, after all we wouldn't want you having an accident when the baby must be due any moment now, would we!'

Terrified and with tears streaming down her face, Maureen pleaded, 'Please, please go away, I'll call the police if you don't.'

Standing behind his brother, Joe McArdle twiddled his lucky silver dollar and said, 'You wouldn't want to go and do that now girly because we might have to hurt your bonny Mammy if you did now,' and he turned and walked off as Pat stepped out of the hall and, followed him down the street whistling nonchalantly.

Trembling, Maureen slammed the door shut and slid home the large bolt before collapsing to her knees, crying uncontrollably. It took her several minutes to regain enough composure to haul herself to her feet and stagger the few feet to the telephone standing on the hall table at the foot of the stairs. Still at home, Jane answered the phone call from her distraught daughter and felt her stomach churn as she listened to her trying through huge sobs, tell her of the McArdles visit and threats.

Fighting to keep her own emotions under control, Jane asked, 'Have you locked the door?'

Sobbing, Maureen replied, 'Yes Mam, should I call the police?'

'No Pet, just you go and sit down, I'll call the police and Terry's work to see if he can come home and I will be there in a few minutes, just go and sit down quietly darling, I'm hanging up now to make those calls.'

Smoking a cigarette with bored detachment, Ginny leant back against the drinks counter behind the bar of the smoke filled, utilitarian and all most empty bar room of the Fell em Doon when Bill breezed in.

Seeing the tall and ruggedly handsome man approaching her, she quickly stubbed out her cigarette and pulling back her shoulders to point her shapely, jumper clad breasts at him, she pouted her red lips and asked, in what she thought was her sexiest voice, 'Yes Pet, what can I get you?'

Looking intently at the heavily made up but still pretty and shapely Ginny, Bill thought, 'A little less make up and she would be a real looker,' before replying, 'I'll have a small whisky please.'

When she placed the small tumbler of whisky in front of him, he asked, 'Are you Ginny then Pet?'

Flattered that he knew her name, she made a show of smoothing down her black skirt before replying, 'Yes I am, why what can Aah do for you?'

Taking a small sip of whisky, he leaned forward and said quietly, 'I'm Bill Armstrong, Nick Shepherd's cousin and I'm here to find out what happened to him and was hoping you could tell me something about his last week.'

Taken by surprise, Ginny put her hand to her mouth and stood gaping at Bill for several seconds as he put down his drink and said, 'I'm sorry if it's a shock, if you want I can come back later?'

She shook her head and replied, 'No, it's alright, I just thought that part of me life was finished with, you took me by surprise that's all but you must have read all aboot it in the papers?'

'No I haven't, I was in the jungle in Malaya when it happened and I've just got back from the Far East, my mother has told me most of it but as he was living with you at the end, I thought you might be able to tell me what happened on that last day and what the McArdles were up to?'

Ginny grimaced when she heard the McArdles name and said, 'Look it's very quiet today so I can tell you what happened but Aah'll hev to serve any body that wants owt while am telling ye.' Bill nodded as she continued, 'Aah think it was them McArdles that caused the bother; they put Nick under so much pressure that he cracked up man, he couldn't handle their threats and was terrified all the time.'

Bill listened intently as Ginny told him of that last fateful day when Nick had returned to her flat drunk and continued to drink until he passed out an hour before the Grand National was run and how when she woke him he had drunk even more as he listened to the race and had become uncontrollably distraught when the horse the McArdles had bet on, won. She told him of Nick storming out saying he was going to get some money he had hidden at his home in the Sixth Row and how a few minutes later he had come back covered in blood, snatched his petty cash bag, hit her with it when she asked him to stay and then run out again, bumping into the McArdles who had come looking for their money.

Bill interrupted her, 'My Mam has told me what happened after that, so you believe if the McArdles had not come onto the scene Nick would not have gotten into trouble?'

She nodded, 'I'm positive; me and Nick were planning wor lives together, iviry thing was ganning fine until they showed up and forced him to tek their big bet and ruined everything.'

'But what about his wife and kids Ginny?'

'He told me he was ganning te leave them as they all hated him!'

Bill rubbed his chin and said, 'Thanks for that Ginny, it's more or less what I thought, am sorry if I upset you I just wanted to be sure of me facts.'

She nodded and looking at his empty glass said, 'That's okay, do you want another drink?'

'Aye go on, I will and you can tell me more about the McArdles.' Ginny told him everything she knew of the two brothers, of where they lived and rumours of their other illegal activities but she did not tell him of her having got rid of Nick's baby with a back street abortion nor of the money she received from a Fleet Street reporter for her story that had enabled her to move into a new flat!

After Maureen hung up, Jane immediately telephoned Ashington Police Station and asked for Detective Sergeant Norman but was disappointed when she was told he was out on another case. Remembering that he had told her that uniform would not take any action unless the McArdles actually broke the law, she asked them to leave a message for him to contact her when he returned and hung up.

It took a couple of minutes before she got through to Terry and began explaining what was happening but Terry cut her off with, 'I'm on me way hyem noo!'

Terrified that the McArdles might still be hanging round, she telephoned Edward's home hoping he would be there for lunch. He was and answered the telephone on the third ring, saying through a mouthful of stottie and ham, 'Hello, Thompson Electrics.'

He listened intently as Jane quickly explained what had happened and asked if he could come round, to which he replied as calmly as he could, 'I'm on my Jane, wait until I get there, I'll be two minutes.'

Wearing his navy blue working overalls, he rushed outside and climbed into his Commer van and drove quickly up Wansbeck Road, across the Store and Corner, around the Plantation into High Market where he saw the McArdles standing smoking in the alley that led to the back of the White House Club! Braking sharply, he pulled the van up behind Bill's Triumph that was still parked outside Jane's house and stormed back toward the McArdles, who, realising there was going to be a confrontation, flicked their cigarettes away as he approached.

Bill had enjoyed his talk with Ginny who he had noticed, had become a little flirtatious as their conversation changed to other subjects, until he reluctantly left and walked back toward his car, reaching Willington's Newsagents where he saw Edward screech to a halt and rush toward the White House. Recognising Edward immediately, he wondered why he was in such a hurry until he saw the McArdles backing into the alley between the White House and Plantation and he realised there was going to be trouble.

Seeing Edward approaching menacingly, the McArdles stepped further back until they were out of view of anyone on the street and waited.

Edward stormed after them and spat, 'Right you two gutless blidy cowards, now yer threatening a pregnant lass as well as a woman on her an, I'm telling you that it ends here and now, ye'll clear off and never come back!'

Unflinching, Pat sneered at Edward, 'Brave words Mista but seeing as how yer on yer own, just how are you going to make us leave?'

Reaching into his jacket pocket with his right hand, Joe pulled out a rubber clad lead cosh and swinging it threateningly, growled, 'Come on then big fella, let's see what yer made of.'

The McArdles were smaller and heavier than Edward but as neither of them had done a day's hard work in their lives; much of their bulk was fat, whereas Edward was lean, muscular and not afraid of them but was not sure what underhand tricks they would pull in the alley and said quietly, 'There will be no need for violence if you leave now.'

'Too late laddie,' Pat snapped and swung a powerful kick that missed as Edward neatly side-stepped and caught him with a hard swinging left hook that rattled Pat's teeth but did not slow him. Pat threw himself forward trying to grab Edward as Joe raised the cosh and stepped around trying to get a clear swing at Edward who was throwing punches at Pat. Joe's first wild swing missed Edward's head by inches, smacking instead heavily onto his shoulder. Joe stepped back and raised the cosh for another swing but before he could, the mighty left hand of Bill Armstrong grabbed his wrist and twisted it violently, forcing him to drop the cosh as Bill spun him round and smashed a powerful right into the face of the shocked crook, knocking him onto his back semi-conscious.

With Joe down, Edward quickly battered Pat to his knees and using his foot, pushed him onto his back before turning to see who had come to his assistance, 'My God, it's Bill, isn't it?'

Nodding, Bill replied, 'Aye Eddie, I thought I better step in before you did too much damage to these two rats!'

Sitting with his legs apart and with his senses slowly returning, Joe tried to sit up but Bill stepped forward and kicked him in the groin with enough force to propel him backwards into the fence, where moaning loudly, he curled up foetus like.

Realising he and his brother were outmatched, Pat held his hands up to protect his battered face and begged, 'Enough, we've had enough!'

Edward stood over the brothers and warned, 'I will not tell you swine again, get out of High Market and divvint come back, in fact get oot of Ashington and stay away or so help me I will swing for the pair of you.'

Bill added, 'Just in case yer wondering who I am; I'm Nick Shepherd's cousin and I hold you two partly responsible for what happened to him. Now that you've been fettled, I'll leave it at that but if you know what's good for you, you'll stay away from here,' then turning to Edward, he said, 'Come on Eddie, I don't think they'll dare show their faces around here again.'

'Thanks Bill, I've got te go and see Jane, Nick's wife, them bastards threatened her pregnant daughter and she's distraught.'

With an angry look, Bill responded 'I spoke to Jane earlier and she told me of the bother they had been causing her, you go and see her and I'll make sure these two buggers clear off.'

As Edward went in to comfort Jane, Bill turned around and watched the McArdles limp out of the alley, Pat supporting Joe who had one hand clutching his battered groin. They turned left and headed for the door of the Club but Bill walking toward them shaking his head was enough for the pair to turn around and hobble back toward their car parked outside the Portland Hotel with Bill following them all the way.

Opening the door to Edward's knock, Jane grabbed his arm saying, 'Thanks Edward, I was afraid to walk round to Maureen's in case the McArdles were waiting.'

'They were lass but they have been sent on their way by Bill Armstrong and me, I doubt ye'll hear from them again,' he said as he led her out to the van.

She stopped and looking at his face noticed a slight redness under his left eye, 'Oh you haven't been fighting Edward, I would hate it if you got into trouble because of them.'

Opening the van door for her smiled, 'Not so much as a fight, more teaching them a lesson Pet.' Turning the van round, he drove back toward Maureen's passing the McArdles with Bill a few yards behind as they limped past the Holy Sepulchre Church.

Terry ran the half mile from the Mining College and finding the door locked, knocked hard shouting, 'It's me Maureen, let me in.'

Opening the door, she fell into his arms sobbing and clung onto him for dear life just as Edward drove up with Jane, the two of them hurrying into the house after Terry and Maureen. While Terry comforted his distraught teenage wife, Jane explained what had happened, Terry becoming angrier by the second until he snarled, 'That's it, I'll tell me Dad and we'll gan after the wasters and sort them oot once and for all!'

'There's no need to Terry Lad,' said Edward, 'Bill Armstrong and me have given them a bit of a hiding and I cannit see them coming roond here again after that.'

Shaking his head, Terry said, 'Nur, they need fettling for good and me and my Dad will de it!'

Jane said worriedly, 'Now Terry, you cannot get yourself into trouble, not with the baby due next week, you need to be here to look after Maureen, the McArdles are just not worth getting into trouble over.'

A calmer Maureen added, 'Mam's right Terry, I don't want to see you in trouble or them swine hurting you, if they come back we should leave them to the police.'

Jane added, 'She's right Terry, we should leave it to the police and I have asked them to have Sergeant Norman telephone me when he returns from another matter.'

Detective Sergeant Jamie Norman did not receive the message from Jane until three o'clock that afternoon and after calling her without receiving an answer, he drove the half mile down to High Market and parked his Ford Anglia outside of Kirkup's Bakery. Seeing him pull up,

Jane rushed outside and took him along to her house where she explained what had happened.

Listening intently, he scribbled a few notes before saying, 'This has gone far enough Jane, I will go and find the McArdles now and give them their final warning and tell them to stay out of Ashington, I hope young Maureen is not too upset and that you are over the shock but please, when you next see Edward Thompson, tell him not to take the law into his own hands again as it could backfire.' They talked for another ten minutes before he left to track down the brothers and Jane returned to work.

Finding no sign of the McArdles black Ford Prefect outside any of the pubs or clubs, the last one being the White Elephant at the south end of Ashington, he drove down and across the Stakeford Bridge over the Wansbeck, past West Sleekburn to their caravan standing bleakly amongst scrub in its windswept position overlooking the estuary. Noting that their car was parked next to a couple of wrecks he stopped on the tarmac road and walked gingerly through the accumulated rubbish strewn haphazardly around the long, green caravan and knocked loudly on the door.

Sporting a black eye and swollen lip, Pat flung the door open and demanded, 'What the blidy hell de you want copper?'

Looking up at the dishevelled and battered crook, Jamie Norman grinned and replied, 'I want a word with you and your brother, can I come in?'

Twiddling his lucky silver dollar, Joe joined his brother at the door of the caravan and not wanting the Detective to see the boxes of contraband whisky they had stacked at one end of the caravan, barked, 'No ye cannot, if you have anything to say, you can say it from there!'

Glaring at them Jamie said loudly and firmly with his Scottish lilt, 'You two have overstepped the mark this time, now I'm warning the pair of you, stay away from Ashington or I'll come after you.'

Pat laughed mockingly, 'We've done nuting wrong copper and a lanky piece of Scotch shite like you doesn't scare us laddie, now piss off and bother somebody you can handle!'

Just managing to control his anger, Jamie retorted, 'I've warned you, stay away from Mrs Trevelyan and her family or so help me I will hunt you down myself and hurt you.'

'So that's it,' Joe sneered, 'You fancy the wida Shepherd or Trevelyan or whatever she's calling herself, mind she has got a lovely arse and me and my brother here fancy some of that now.'

Fuming, Jamie spat, 'I coming after you two pieces of scum, I have warned you,' and turned to walk away as the McArdles taunted him with their mocking laughter.

Terry did not go back to work that afternoon but did walk round to the Third Row and over a cup of tea, relay the events of earlier in the day to his increasingly angry father.

The rough justice they received from Edward and Bill and the warning they had from DS Jamie Norman did not appear to have had any effect on the brothers as they drove slowly through High Market before spending the night taking bets and drinking in the Grand Hotel and Comrades Working Men's Club. Driving home at ten forty, they were totally unaware that a car was following them at a discreet distance and later as they sat drinking whisky inside the caravan, they were oblivious of the shadowy figure prowling silently around the outside of their caravan and lurking in the shadows of a half-moon. The watcher waited until just after midnight when they climbed into their shabby beds and Joe turned off the gas lamp before he left as silently as he had arrived.

Edward drove around High Market a couple of times the following day looking for any sign of the McArdles but he missed them when they once again cruised through High Market before they toured the clubs again that night and were once more followed back to their caravan without them being aware that someone was stalking them.

The following morning, Friday the twelfth of September dawned wet and windy as Bill, fresh from his morning walk packed his car whilst his Mother made him sandwiches and a flask of tea for his journey asking, 'What time are ye catching the ferry Bill?'

'Tomorrow morning Mam, so I'll have a slow drive down today and find a B and B in Dover for the night, hopefully I will see Wilhelm on Sunday and I should be back on Tuesday morning all being well.'

Shortly after returning home from school, Howard and Jake cycled round to Hotspur House and Met up with Ian and Rafe in the garden to discuss what time they were all going to set off for the Battle of Britain Air Show at Acklington the following day.

Ian said, 'We'll leave here at half past nine,' and turning to Jake, warned, 'So mek sure yer here Jake or we'll leave you.'

Grinning, Jake replied, 'Aye nee bother man, anyway wore Ronnie's ganning in his car and he offered te tek me and me Mam and Dad but Aah telt him Aah was ganning we ye lot and me Mam said she's staying hyem with Billy and Roger as they hev cowlds and me Dad says he'll be working in his shed.'

Looking puzzled, Rafe asked, 'What has Ronnie driving to the Air Show got to do with you not being here on time Jake?'

'Aah just meant if Aah was late and am not saying Aah will be, Aah can gan te the show in the car we Ronnie like!'

'That's it,' snapped Howard, 'the little sod cannit be bothered te bike ower te Acklington, he wants te travel by car!'

Feigning affront, Jake replied, 'Whey nur man, I want te bike ower we ye lot it's ownly haf a dozen miles noo init?'

Rafe put his arm around Jake, 'Then you are probably hoping to see Julia before you leave, is that it Jake me lad?'

Blushing and very embarrassed, Jake responded with, 'Hadaway te hell man, why on urth wud Aah hang aboot for a lass?'

'Cos ye fancy her and she's been flashing her smile at ye,' said Howard.

Their banter was cut short when Mike pulled into the drive on his James motorcycle that did not sound as though it was running smoothly.

Ian waited until he had dismounted and taken off his crash helmet before asking, 'Are ye ganning to the Air Show tomorrow Mike?'

He shook his head, 'Nah, I've football training in the morning and I'm taking my bike round to Jake's dad in the afternoon to see if he can sort out the carburettor for me in time to pop over to Morpeth to see Jennifer.'

As the lads chatted the McArdles drove slowly past in their battered black Ford, turning off and parking at the end of the Eigth Row where they could watch Hotspur House through their rear view mirror. They sat there until just after six o'clock and then drove round to the Portland, parking up outside before strolling in to begin their evening drinking and taking under the table bets. Finishing the night at the Grand, they were both verging on drunkenness when they climbed into their car at eleven o'clock to drive back to their caravan. They weren't followed but as they pulled up next to the caravan, a shadowy figure dressed in dark overalls and wearing gloves, hunched down behind one of the abandoned cars as dark clouds blotted out the moon and stars turning their patch stygian black!

Once inside, Joe, turned on the gas and lit the mantle above the forward seating area and waited as the gas lamp heated and slowly spluttered into a bright light. Pat had already opened the bottle of whisky that they had left on the table between the two shabby bench seats and pouring two large measures into grubby tumblers, he passed one to his brother.

'Here you go Joe; we might as well finish the bottle while we figure out what we're going to do about the wida Shepherd.'

Throwing his jacket on the bench, Joe took the whisky and downing it one gulp replied, 'I think we'll give her a wee visit on Monday and we'll take sumting to fettle that blidy Edward fella if he's about.'

Pouring more whisky, Pat asked, 'What about that fucking giant, Nick's cousin who knocked you down Joe?'

Lighting a cigarette, Joe replied, 'Well now, as ye know we found out he's a soldier boy so I wud think we won't see much of him so we'll just make sure he's not about before we make our move.'

While the brothers continued to smoke and drink, the shadowy figure outside picked up a two foot long, heavy steel bar that he had chosen earlier from the scrap lying scattered around the caravan and stealthily walked to where the light shone through the grubby net curtains of the front side window and stood silently, listening.

By twelve o'clock the brothers were drunk and discussing in obscene detail what they were going to do to Jane when a loud rap on the door startled them.

Lounging back against the front of the caravan where he was playing with his lucky silver dollar, Joe, snapped, 'Who the fuck's that at this time of night, I bet it's that fucking sailor boy wanting more blidy money for his whisky, go and tell him to fuck off Pat.'

Pat lurched to his feet and staggered drunkenly to the door in the middle of the van where, steadying himself he flung it open and leaning out shouted, 'Fuck off!'

Standing in deep shadow to one side of the door the figure swung the metal bar at Pat's stomach causing him to bend double and pitch head first out of the caravan where he landed with a thud in front of the wraith like figure who, stepped swiftly over Pat, placed his knee into the squealing Irishman's back and grabbing his head with both hands pulled back and twisted with brutal force, snapping his neck and killing him instantly.

Seeing his brother disappear screaming through the door, Joe struggled to climb off the bench where he had been sprawled and staggered to his feet as the overall clad intruder stepped inside, stopping joe in his tracks, 'You,' he snapped, 'What the fuck are you doing here, where's Pat?'

Squinting in the gas light, the intruder advanced menacingly toward Joe and growled, 'Pat's dead and I'm here to kill you!'

Realising the danger he was in, Joe, flicked his silver dollar at the intruder and tried to rush him but instead he ran straight into the swinging metal bar that smashed into his face, breaking his nose and cheek bone, stopping him in his tracks as the other man pushed him violently back onto the bench and hit him with three more crushing blows to his head, smashing his skull, splattering blood, bone and brains across the bench and table.

Panting heavily the man checked Joe for a pulse and finding none, he then went about breaking and throwing the loose contents of the caravan around before dropping the bar next to Joe. Calmly walking outside, he with some difficulty, lifted Pat over his shoulder and carried him to the McArdle's car; opening the passenger door and lowering the dead man onto the seat. Returning to the caravan he picked up the car keys from the kitchen sink drainer where Joe had left them and noticing something shining on the floor he bent down to pick up Joe's lucky silver dollar and looked at briefly before shoving it into his trouser pocket.

Taking two bottles of whisky from a box at the other end of the caravan he pushed one into his pocket and opened the other, pouring half of it over Joe and then splashing the rest over the seating area and kitchen before discarding the bottle. Reaching up, he turned off the burning gas mantle and waited quietly until it had cooled down before he took a cigarette from a packet he had taken from the table and lit it with a Joe's lighter. Taking two long drags, he dropped the burning cigarette on the floor by the door where it lay smouldering and reaching up, he turned the gas mantle back on and quickly stepped outside, walked to the car and climbed in.

Driving slowly away, he pulled onto the tarmac road and headed toward Ashington as the sky in his rear view mirror erupted in a yellow flash when the smouldering cigarette ignited the gas escaping from the mantle in a ball of flame that quickly engulfed the caravan, the conflagration made worse by exploding whisky bottles and finally two gas bottles that totally destroyed the caravan.

Rain began to fall gently as he drove slowly through West Sleekburn, across Stakeford Bridge, turning up North Seaton Road and left in to Green Lane to drive past Ashington Farm toward Sheepwash just as the first Police car arrived at the destroyed caravan followed a few minutes later by two fire engines.

He slowed as he approached the crumbling tarmac track that ran into the woods bordering the north side of the river Wansbeck and switching off the car lights, he turned onto the track and crawled slowly along passing the remains of a broken and discarded five bar gate that still had a large and barely legible sign that read, 'Keep Out – Danger deep water'.

This was the access track to the water filled old quarry that had produced stone for the many large houses and farms in the area. The quarry had not been used for fifty years and slowly filling with water, it had been used as a dumping pit for years even after the council had fenced it off when a young boy had drowned when he fell into its murky depths.

He drove slowly the fifty yards to the remains of a dilapidated single strand and totally ineffectual barbed wire fence that marked the edge of the quarry where numerous cars had been parked over the years while their owners threw scrap into the deep water below. Leaving the engine running, he opened the front windows of the car and then stepping out, he reached back in to heave the lifeless Pat McArdle into the driver's seat. Satisfied that the body was in position he took the bottle of whisky from his pocket, opened it and poured some over the front of the body and then wedged the bottle in between it and the car seat. Releasing the hand brake he pushed the car a few yards until the momentum of the slope took over and the car ran forward, snapping the rusty barbed wire as it careered over the edge of the quarry, dropping ten foot and splashing into the dark, deep water where it settled for a few seconds before slowly sinking out of view.

Waiting until bubbles from the now totally submerged car stopped escaping, he then listened quietly for a few more moments before walking back to the Sheepwash Road where he stopped to look around before taking off his overall and gloves, rolling them up and tucking them under his arm as he walked briskly away.

He walked back along a wet Green Lane that glistened under street lamps, down a deserted North Seaton Road and into Jubilee Trading Estate where he had discreetly parked his car earlier in the evening. Unlocking the car, he climbed in and breathed slowly out in attempt to drain the tension from his stress tightened muscles before starting his car and carefully driving off.

Chapter Eight
Consequences

The overnight rain had stopped and a light breeze had chased away the darker clouds, leaving only the occasional large cotton wool ball drifting slowly across a clear blue sky as Jake cycled back from having completed his Saturday morning paper-round. Despite the warmth of the mid-September morning, the air was thick from the smoke of freshly stoked or newly lit coal fires as the folk in the 'Ra's' rose to enjoy Saturday, the best day of the week for most. Wearing his leather jacket, white tee shirt and denim jeans and with his hair slicked back with Brylcreem, Jake was certainly in a good mood; he believed he looked super cool and looked forward to strutting round RAF Acklington impressing any girls that were bound to be there.

Reaching home, he propped his bike against the yard fence, then walking into the kitchen, he found Billy and Roger at the table eating toast while their mother Flo stood in front of the fire toasting another slice on the long wire handled toasting fork.

Jake grabbed a slice from a protesting Roger, who complained with a sniff, 'Mam wor Jake's pinched me toast!'

Without turning Flo snapped, 'I'll skelp your bloody lugs Jake, leave the bairns alen.'

Through a mouthful of mashed toast, he grinned at his two younger brothers and asked, 'Are ye two ganning te the air-show we Ronnie?'

Before they could answer, Flo said, 'Nur we cannit hev them snotting aall ower Mary can we, they'll bide here but if tha any better the sefternoon they can bugger of to the pictures!'

Wearing a collarless shirt, slippers, braces dangling and newspaper tucked underneath his arm, Albert walked in from his morning visit to the netty and asked, 'Who's ganning te the pictures, Aah thought them two buggas had cowlds?'

Flo dropped the bread she had toasted on Roger's plate and began buttering it saying, 'These two aren't exactly at Death's Door are they, it'll get them oot the hoose and from under my feet if they want te gan.'

Shoving another piece of bread onto the toasting fork she returned to the fire as Roger reached for his toast but was beaten to it by his Dad, '*Oh Dad man,*' he complained, 'Mam me Dad's eating me toast noo, am sick of this, am starving ye kna.'

Flo turned on Albert with the toasting fork, 'Ye greedy skinny little bugga ye, fancy pinching the bairns toast, Aah'll shove this blidy fork right up yer Jacksy in a blidy minute!

Howard, who had just arrived, stepped into the kitchen and said, 'Ne toast for me Mrs Grundy. Howeh Jake are ye ready?

Tapping Billy on the right side of his head, Jake reached around to Billy's left as he turned and grabbing his half eaten piece of toast, quickly made for the door replying, 'Aye come on, I'll niver get a piece of toast here,' and hurried out as the toasting fork clattered on the door behind him.

An hour and a half later all five of the Hacky Dortys were cycling past the queue of traffic lined up waiting to enter RAF Acklington. The area around the entrance to the show was organised chaos as the RAF Police tried to ensure that cars followed the circuit to the car parking area, while directing those on bikes or on foot to the display area. The lads weaved in and out of cars, other cyclists and past the RAF Police who waved at them to dismount but who they ignored before they were clear of the crush.

They eventually followed a man on a bike with a young boy sitting on a seat fastened to his crossbar, Ian asking him, 'Is this the right way Mister?'

The tall handsome man beamed at them and replied, 'Yes lads, just follow me and I'll show you where you can leave yor bikes.'

'Cor look at this lot,' said Jake a few minutes later when they walked in between two huge hangars and onto a large open area lined on both sides with aeroplanes of all shapes and sizes.

As Jake and Roger made for a parked Sycamore helicopter, Rafe said to Ian, 'I'm going over to the Hawker Hunters; I believe you can have your photo taken sitting inside the cockpit.'

Ian nodded and looking across at the fighters replied, 'Okay, then I want to have a look at the Canberra and Mosquito.'

Howard added, I want te look at the lot, just as well we hev aall day like.'

As the crowds grew, Jake and Roger looked around the Sycamore Helicopter, Jake asking the Pilot, 'Any chance of ganning up in one of these Mista?'

Smiling down at Jake, he answered, 'Sorry son, there will be no flights for spectators but you will see a flying elephant later on that you might find fun!'

Looking at the Pilot as if he had lost his senses, Jake retorted, 'A flying elephant, your crackers man, elephants divvint fly de they!'

'They do here lad, just wait and see.'

Grabbing Jake by the arm, Roger said, 'Howay lets gan and hev a look at the jets man and look ower there, tha's some soldiers and army stuff.'

Waiting their turn to climb into the Hawker Hunter fighter, Rafe and Ian looked across at the runway as three Gloster Meteor, twin jet engine Fighters took off, climbing swiftly before heading south just as a formation of two huge Valiants and a massive delta winged Vulcan flew down the length of the runway then turned and flew back individually, the commentator describing the role of the mighty bombers over the public address system.

After he had his photograph taken sitting in the cockpit, Rafe climbed down and approached an immaculately dressed Squadron Leader with several medal ribbons below his wings, asking him politely, 'Excuse me Sir, but can you tell me what qualifications I would need to become a pilot?'

The Officer turned and looked the tall, handsome Rafe up and down, noting the grey trousers, expensive open-necked shirt and cricket pullover draped casually around his shoulders before smiling and asking, 'I suppose you mean a fighter pilot?'

'Well, yes I suppose so, although I would be happy just to be a pilot.'

'Judging from your accent, you are not from around here, are you?'

Rafe smiled, 'I am now Sir but until earlier this year I lived just outside Coventry.'

'Education, is what you need first my boy, you will need a good batch of 'A' levels or a degree if you want to become an RAF Officer.'

'I do Sir and I do intend to go to University.'

'Excellent,' the Officer replied, 'some Universities have RAF Officer Cadets so you should consider taking that route.'

While Rafe chatted to the RAF Officer and Ian posed inside the cockpit, the other three lads laughed and joked as they watched the flying elephant display - a Whirlwind helicopter with two huge eyes painted on the front with a trunk dangling in between. It flew low along the runaway, swaying from side to side, wagging the trunk as it did so. This was followed by a magnificent fly past of twelve delta winged Gloster Javelin all weather fighters that brought cheers and applause from the thousands of spectators who now lined the run way and crowded around the static displays.

The five lads met up at the far end of the display area where the Royal Northumberland Fusiliers had set up a recruiting display against a large Commer truck. A Sergeant and Corporal wearing green combat clothing and the brand new 1958 pattern webbing were demonstrating a variety of weapons, including the new Self Loading Rifle, General Purpose Machine Gun and, the Light Machine Gun based upon the old Bren Gun. Jake was clearly impressed by the way the soldiers were turned out and their confident manner and was soon examining the weapons in detail.

Taking an interest in the boys the Sergeant said, 'Right lads, watch as I strip this LMG down to its five main parts and resemble it,' which he did smoothly and efficiently before asking, 'Okay, who wants to try that?'

Howard stepped forward, saying, 'Me, I can de that,' but having not fully grasped the demonstration, he quickly became confused on what to do next and had to be guided through the procedure.

When Howard finished, Jake asked, 'Can I have a go please?'

Ian looked at Jake and said, 'Blidy hell Jake, that's the forst time I've hurd ye say please.'

While the Sergeant made room for him, Jake replied, 'Aye whey Aah can say it when Aah need to.' Then much to the other lads astonishment, Jake slowly and methodically dismantled the machine gun and after smiling mockingly at Howard, quickly reassembled it as the other lads turned to head back toward the runway and flying display.

Jake remained behind and watched as the Sergeant demonstrated how to strip and assemble the Self-Loading Rifle.

'Go on then son have a go at that.' He did and with only one prompt as the Sergeant watched with interest before saying, 'You're not as daft as you make out are you lad?'

'Whey Aah like making people laff like!'

Taking Jake to one side, the Sergeant said, 'It's good to have a laugh son but make sure people are laughing with you not at you, now how long have you got left at school?'

'Aah leave next March.'

'And what are you going to do with yourself then?'

'Doon the pit Aah suppose but me brother is in the army, he's just come back from Singapore and he keeps telling me hoo great it is, so I was thinking aboot joining up when am owld enough.'

Smiling, the Sergeant asked, 'Who is your brother with then?'

'The Northumbrian Borderers,'

'We'll forgive him that eh, but you can join the Boy's Army when you are fifteen, did you know that?'

Jake listened intently as the Sergeant told him about the Junior Soldier's Army that consisted of many different Regiments and Corps; that the infantry had a Junior Infantry Regiment, while other Corps had Junior Leaders and Junior Tradesmen Regiments and that he could serve in the Junior Army until he was seventeen and a half when he would move to the Army proper. He also explained that Jake could gain promotion with the Junior Army up to the Rank of Junior Regimental Sergeant Major but would have to revert to Private when he joined mans' Army.

Soaking up the information Jake said, 'Thanks Sergeant, Aah fancy the soond of Junior Leader like,' and ran off to catch up with the others.

Having showered at the Welfare after football practice, Mike arrived home just before lunch and found Tommy building a plastic 'Airfix' Spitfire model on the kitchen table, 'Alright Tom what ye doing this afternoon?'

His tongue sticking out with concentration, Tommy carefully laid the half-finished model down and answered, 'I was going roond te Billy and Roger's te see if they are ganning te the Regal te see "The Vikings," it's supposed te be great.'

Mike nodded, 'So I hear, I'll give ye a lift roond on my motorbike, tha dad is going te hev a look at me carburettor.'

An hour later, after eating the hot pies their mother had brought them, Mike waited until Tommy climbed onto the back of his motor bike and then drove off down High Market past the White House, turning left down the road that led toward the colliery. This road was flanked on the left by the gable ends and gardens of the First to Sixth Rows and on the right by the Seventh to Tenth Rows. Mike turned left down the Fifth Row and rode slowly down to the end of the second terrace before taking the diagonal rode past the Scouts hut at the foot of the 'Rec' Bridge where a gang of kids were re-enacting the Battle of the Alamo and into the second terrace of the Sixth Row, past a Butcher's delivery horse and cart and across the gap to the third terrace before pulling up next to Albert Grundy's air-raid shelter, cum shed, cum workshop.

Mike switched off as Albert, wearing his greasy overalls and wiping his hands on an even greasier rag, stepped out of the brick shed, took the fag end of his bottom lip and said, 'Alreet lads; hev ye come te see Billy and Roger then Tommy lad?

Tommy nodded, 'Aye Mr Grundy, are they ganning te the pictures?'

Albert replied, 'Whey they've had cowld but Aah think that Flo might want them oot the hoose, she's already hoyed them inte the garden, go on in and see,' and turning to Mike he said, 'start her up again Mike so Aah can hear her ticking ower.'

Mike kicked the engine back into spluttering life as Aggie Galloway who had been in the Turnbull's house delivering a large bag of potatoes that her husband Arthur had dug out of his garden that morning, cantered up.

Grabbing Tommy just before he made it into the Grundy's yard, she planted a smacking wet kiss on his cheek, saying, 'Eee yer looking as handsome as iver bonny lad,' before continuing on to her yard and a natter with Mary Holland, her next door neighbour.

Wiping his face Tommy wondered why she had said it as though it had been ages since she had seen him and not the night before when she had delivered a bag of potatoes to his mother!

Although she loved her dearly and was very grateful for her support, Irene Turnbull had been glad when Aggie had finally left. Aggie had brought the potatoes just after lunch while Irene was organising her four older bairns for a trip to the beach at Newbiggin with their Dad who was holding Max the Border Collie who strained on the leash to go. After they left, Aggie had helped her clear away the lunch plates before sitting down for a cup of tea in the kitchen while two year old Raymond annoyed his four year old brother Robert who was trying to complete a large piece jigsaw on the sitting room floor. It was baby Rosalind crying to be fed that finally prompted Aggie to leave, saying, 'Aah'll get from under yer feet lass and let ye feed the baby, scuttling out as Mike and Tommy had rode past on Mike's motorbike.

Flying in formation one thousand feet above Morpeth, the three Gloster Meteors that had taken off earlier from RAF Acklington followed the line of the river Wansbeck east toward Ashington as they waited to be called back to complete their demonstration over the airfield.

From the cockpit of the left hand jet of the three, Flying Officer Hugh Harley asked the formation leader, 'Permission to buzz my girl's house skipper?'

Flight Lieutenant Mark Renshaw replied, 'Go ahead, we've plenty of time, re-join us over Newbiggin Bay but stay above two hundred feet.'

Like a boisterous dog let of its leash, Hugh banked sharply to his left, pushed his Meteor into a shallow dive and hurtled toward Ashington and levelling off at 100 feet, he roared over his madly waving girlfriend in the garden of one of the large houses in Green lane before flying north over the Colliery Rows and then over the Colliery itself, aiming slightly west to avoid the massive pit heaps.

Preparing for their engagement party that evening, Wendy Robson had not gone to the air show and had walked into the centre of her parent's garden at one thirty, just as Hugh had suggested she should. With the sound of the jet receding as it hurtled north, she hurried back inside, thrilled at having seen her glamorous boyfriend fly over and grinned as her mother shook her head. Hugh had swept her off her feet just twelve months before when he joined his Squadron at RAF Acklington where she worked in the Headquarters Building. She had turned down several other Officers who had tried to court her but the dashing Hugh was different, he was the one for her and she looked forward to their wedding next summer but first the engagement party.

Having the time of his life, Hugh thought, 'Time for one more pass, then re-join the flight.'

Dropping down to fifty feet and banking sharply to his right until the Jet was flying on its right-hand side, he swung it sharply around the three old pit heaps, aiming to fly between them and the one that was currently in use before flying low back over Green Lane. Still flying on his side he entered the gap and gasped involuntarily when he saw the aerial ropeway carrying the buckets of slag across the opening to be dumped on the new heap; it was at least a hundred feet above his current flight path! Trying desperately to level the jet and climb, he hurtled toward it at three hundred miles an hour realising with inevitable certainty and dread that he could not hope to avoid it.

Mike and Albert had heard the roar of the Meteor's twin Rolls Royce Derwent engines when it had flown over the Rows and stood listening and waiting, hearing it turn in the distance and head back toward Ashington, Albert commenting, 'By that bugga's flying low!'

Standing outside her house at the top of the Row gossiping with Mary Holland, Aggie also commented on the low flying jet, 'Tha's nee caall for them te be flying that low roond here noo is tha?'

Still flying tipped over on his right as he tried desperately level off and climb, Hugh felt the jolt of the impact with the steel ropeway through the joystick as the right wing outside of the engine was neatly sheared off, causing the jet to dip and swing to the right as he tried frantically to turn the crippled aeroplane away from Ashington.

Losing height and stability, he calmly called, 'Mayday, Mayday, Mayday,' into his microphone as he managed to bring the jet round a little, hoping to eject once he knew he had turned away from the Colliery Rows but the slim concrete upper super structure of the 'Rec' Bridge stood in the way!

The fuselage just cleared the top but the already damaged right wing was ripped clean off as it smacked into the long beam that ran along the top of the bridge's superstructure, causing the jet to begin to cartwheel toward the Sixth Row.

Spewing burning aviation fuel, the ripped off wing with the engine still attached slammed into a long line of coal filled railway wagons running parallel to the Sixth Row, engulfing three of them in a huge fire ball and igniting the wooden wagons and the coal inside. It was too late for Hugh to eject as the intact left wing of the cartwheeling aircraft was torn off by the outside toilets and coalhouses of the second Sixth Row terrace. Smashing into the concrete and brick outhouses, it demolished several of them, exploding in another ball of flame, the explosion blowing out most of the windows in the row, stampeding the Butcher's horse and cart toward the Scout Hut where the kids were playing and sending the Butcher and a customer running for cover.

The second strike had slowed the now wingless fuselage as it completed its somersault, collapsing part of the end gable of the second Sixth Row and slamming tail first and upside down into the houses of the third Terrace; knocking down part of the gable wall and roof of the Turnbull's house before exploding into numerous pieces as it completely demolished the next three houses, most of the Grundy's and part of the Williamson's! Part of the tail section sheared off in the impact and hurtling into the Holland's wooden garage at the bottom of their garden, blasted it apart, sending pieces of garage and aircraft flying into the Fifth and Cross Rows.

Hearing the impact of the wing against the 'Rec Bridge', Albert had stood transfixed as he watched the cartwheeling jet hurtle toward him; it was Mike who reacted instinctively, diving at Albert he knocked him back into his air-raid shelter-workshop, landing heavily on top of him as the world outside erupted into an almighty explosion and ball of flame that swept over the second half of the Row to evaporate a hundred feet in the air.

Aggie and Mary Holland had watched the crash in what to them seemed like slow motion; they saw the first wing torn off and explode in a ball of flame then the second erupting across the lower Sixth Row and finally watched in horror as the fuselage demolished half their street, throwing masonry, timber, slates and aircraft debris in all directions, several pieces flying past them, miraculously missing them completely.

In their gardens on the other side of the houses, their husbands George Holland and Arthur Galloway had been sitting on their doorsteps drinking tea and chatting when the first impact compelled them to drop their cups and stand up as the second and third explosions made them duck back down until finally they watched in disbelief as the Holland's Garage exploded into a thousand pieces when the tail piece of the jet slammed into it.

Flying high over Newbiggin Bay, Hugh's 'Mayday' call sent a chill down Flight Lieutenant Mark Renshaw's spine causing him to look west where to his horror, he saw the flash as the first wing exploded into the railway wagons, followed by a second flash as the other wing impacted, then the final ball of flame rising a hundred feet above Ashington to evaporate as two thick clouds of smoke began billing upwards to mingle into one rapidly building black column. Within seconds he was over the crash site, his stomach churning when he recognised parts of the fuselage glinting through the dust and smoke of the third terrace. Trying to remain calm, he called RAF Acklington Control Tower and informed them of what had occurred; repeating his message slowly when they asked him to, 'Please confirm your message!'

As dust and smoke engulfed them inside the sturdily built workshop, Mike rose slowly from his position lying on top of Albert and turned to look at the Maelstrom raging outside; unable to see across the street, he muttered, my God, Tommy, Billy, Roger, Mrs Grundy!' Stepping outside, he coughed as acrid smoke and dust invaded his lungs and blocked his vision causing him to hold his arm up to shield his face as the gentle breeze from the west began to slowly move the smoke and dust toward the Fifth Row.

Standing transfixed and horrified as the air cleared in front of him revealing a scene of devastation, he looked to his right where his motorbike had been blown ten yards down the street and burned fiercely from the fuel spilled from ruptured tank. Turning back he saw that the Grundy's house had been half demolished into a pile of broken walls and smoking rubble with pieces of rafters and beams pointing accusingly skyward. To the right, half of next door had collapsed in on itself and part of the roof of the next house had been damaged. But it was when he looked to the left that he saw the worst, most of the gable end of the Turnbull's at the end of the terrace was still standing but the top floor had been smashed in; the three houses between there and the Grundy's had no recognisable form, having been reduced to a long pile of rubble and aircraft debris, 'There can be no survivors in those three houses,' he thought.

Albert staggered past him toward the remains of his house screaming, 'Me bairns, Flo,' and began climbing desperately up the smouldering heap.

Thinking the boys were still inside, Mike began to move forward when a scared voice stopped him, 'Mike, Mike, we're here,' shouted Tommy from the corner of the street next to the Turnbulls. Looking toward the voice, Mike saw, Tommy and the two Grundy boys standing amongst swirling dust and smoke; none of them appeared to be hurt!

Shouting, 'Mr Grundy the kids are doon here,' Mike ran down to the boys, hugging Tommy and asking, 'where were you?'

'At the corner of the Fifth Row, we'd gone out the front door through the garden and were on wor way te the pictures when we saw the plane come doon.'

Billy grabbed Mike asking, 'Where's me Mam and Dad?'

'Tha alright,' he lied, 'noo ye canna stay here - Tommy, take these two straight round home and call in at Kirkup's and tell Mam what's happened, now go on ye canna stay here it's too dangerous.'

The three boys reluctantly left, passing men and women from the other streets who having heard the crash and seen the smoke rising, were now hurrying to see if they could help.

Albert had not heard Mike and had climbed onto the shattered remains of his home, where despite the fire burning where the kitchen fireplace had been, he was joined by Arthur Galloway and the huge George Holland as he frantically clawed into the wreckage, desperately searching for his family.

Mike was about to run back and join them when a bedraggled and bleeding Alice Turnbull with her baby clutched tightly to her chest, burst out the wreck of her home screaming. 'Me bairns, me bairns!'

Grabbing her and stopping her from trying to hand over her baby to him and rushing back inside, he asked, 'How many are in there?'

Wild eyed and filthy with dust, she stared at him almost uncomprehendingly and shouted, 'Aah was in the kitchen; Raymond and Robert, they wor in the sitting room in front of the fire!

Seeing Aggie Galloway and Mary Holloway hurrying toward them, Mike shouted, 'Aggie, look after Mrs Turnbull,' and without thinking, he rushed to the front door that was hanging from its hinges. The area at the foot of the stairs was intact but moving into the kitchen, he saw the ceiling had been collapsed in by part of the gable and a heavy wooden bed stood upright in the middle of the remains of the rafters and other debris. Crouching and scrambling past these, he struggled in the confined space to throw aside a mattress that was blocking the door to the sitting room. Heaving the mattress out of the way, he managed with some difficulty to pull the door open a few inches. Peering into what had been the sitting room; he took a deep breath when he saw that the upper floor complete with bedroom furniture and some rafters had fallen in and appeared to be propped up by the remains of furniture and part of the collapsed outer wall. Above this and looking totally alien, the battered nose of the jet rested on the wall that had separated the Turnbull's house from what had been the house next door!

Thinking it hopeless and that no one could have survived, he was about to leave when he heard a child's voice suddenly scream, 'Mammy.' Kneeling, he peered beneath the collapsed floor and seeing that there were a few inches of space, he instinctively lay down on his belly and wriggled inside as pieces of brick, slate and timber continued to drop from above. Shards of wood, furniture and lumps of debris blocked his way, forcing him to lift and push them aside as he continued to crawl forward inch by inch. Cut and bleeding from broken glass and sharp pieces of wood he reached the remains of the sofa where to one side he could just make out the shape of four year old Robert illuminated by the fire behind him that had been in the fireplace but was now beginning to spread.

Sobbing quietly, Robert saw Mike and began crawling toward him asking, 'Where's me Mammy?'

Reaching out for the boy, Mike gently pulled him toward himself and answered, 'Your Mammy's outside waiting for you, I'll take you out but where's little Raymond?'

Clinging desperately onto Mike's outstretched arms, Robert whispered, 'He's asleep in front of the fire.' Realising there was no space for him to squeeze past Robert; Mike began the slow and painful process of reversing back out; carefully shielding and pulling the little lad as more and more pieces of unstable brickwork fell in.

Once he had reached the kitchen, he was able to crouch and pulled the filthy but unscathed Robert into his arms, scrambling back outside where a distraught Alice Turnbull grabbed her son asking, where's Raymond?'

Wiping dirt and blood from his scratched face and arms, Mike replied, 'I'm going back in for him, just hang on.'

Mary Holland helped Alice with her baby and little Raymond as Aggie grabbed Mike before he could hurry back into the unstable ruin and said, 'Eee look at the state of ye lad, Hang on and Aah'll get George Holland te give ye a hand, they are searching for the poor Grundy bairns and Flo.'

Pulling his arm away from Aggie, Mike said, 'The Grundy lads are alright, tha with Tommy on the way to wore hoose so I think it is just Mrs Grundy inside their hoose. I'm going back in here but see if ye can get a couple of big fellas te come in after me,' and rushed back inside.

Despite fearing what he was going to find and if he would make it safely in and out, Mike unhesitatingly again crawled into the remains of the sitting room as two Ashington Mine Rescue Bedford trucks drove through the smoke billowing down the Rows from the fires of the coal wagons and coal houses and stopped in the centre of the second terrace, just past the fire.

The men quickly dismounted to assess the situation, the Leader ordering 'Ignore the fires to the right until we see if any lives are at risk!'

The spectators at the Air Show noticed that aircraft had begun landing and that the flying programme appeared to have stopped and were beginning to wonder why when the announcer spoke slowly and carefully over the Public Address System, 'Ladies and Gentlemen, your attention please, we have received reports, that most tragically, one of our aircraft has gone down. While we seek to establish the facts we have decided to cancel further flying today. I will update you as soon as we have positive information.'

'Blidy hell, Aah wonder where it's crashed and what it is?' said Jake as the Hacky Dortys turned away from the runway.'

Ian replied, 'Aah don't suppose they'll say out until they know for sure. Unless tha's anything else anybody wants te see we might as well head for home as we're boond te get stuck if everyone tries te leave noo.' The others agreed and the lads headed back to their bikes as scores of spectators headed back to their cars.

They passed Edward Thompson who was walking back to his car with his parents, Ian asking, 'Are ye going Mr Thompson?'

Edward nodded, 'Aye Ian lad were leaving before the rush starts, I'm going to drop me Mam and Dad off in the Sixth Row, I'll see you later, your Mam has invited me roond for tea!'

Jake asked, 'De ye kna where that plane has crashed Mr Thomson?'

'No,' Edward replied, 'They haven't said where yet but it cannit be far away, tragic like if the pilot has been killed!'

Tears cleared streaks down Albert's smoke and dust blackened face as he continued to dig into the rubble and wreckage with increasing fear and frustration. Both his hands were burnt, cut and bleeding but with more men helping, he continued his seemingly hopeless task.

It was George Holland who first tried to drag him away, 'Albert Lad, I think you need to come doon noo, yer hands are in a right mess man!'

Albert brushed George angrily away and half shouted, 'Nur man we've got te get them oot, we've got te keep digging.'

Aggie scuttled up and shouted, 'George can ye come and give young Mike a hand, one of the Turnbull's bairns is trapped?'

Looking down at her he shouted back, 'We're still looking for Albert's bairns and his Mrs man!'

Shocked, Aggie shouted, 'Eeee man, the bairns are not there, tha with young Tommy roond at his hoose, Mike towld me he had seen them.'

Grabbing Albert, George said, 'De ye hear that Albert, yer bairns are alreet man, tha not here?'

Nodding, Albert shook himself free and said, 'Right, thank God Almighty for that but Flo is still here,' and he returned to digging as George climbed down to go to Mike's aid.

Despite more masonry falling into the remains of the room, Mike had managed to crawl back to the settee but was having difficulty wriggling round it. Stopping he called for the missing child, 'Raymond, Raymond, can you hear me?'

There was no answer and calling again, he was rewarded with the sound of a child whimpering and said gently, 'It's alright Raymond, I'm coming to get you, I'm nearly there.' Heaving with all his might, he hauled himself round the front of the settee, scrapping and cutting his back on the shards of rafters as he did so. Crawling forward again, he felt the heat from the fire to his right but he could see Raymond lying on his back just in front of him and reached forward.

Gently grabbing the boy's legs, Mike pulled but stopped when the toddler screamed. Wriggling a little closer, he could see that a piece of rafter had pinned his right arm to the floor. The little lad cried for his mother as Mike squeezed further in until he was almost over the top of him where he paused to gather his strength. After a few seconds he pushed his back up into the collapsed rafters with all his might then struggled to free Raymond's trapped arm. Raymond screamed when the rafters began to move as Mike knelt over him using one hand to drag him free, just as another piece of gable end crashed down on the rafters directly above Mike, collapsing them on top of him, smashing the back of his head and pinning him down in a crouched position over Raymond as the fire slowly spread toward them.

Trying to force his way through the wrecked kitchen of the Turnbull's house, George Holland heaved wreckage out of his way but had to stop twice to protect his head when his efforts dislodged more brickwork from the crumbling outer wall. Eventually, he reached the door to the sitting room which with a mighty heave, he forced open enough to look inside.

Seeing the collapsed upper floor piled with rafters and debris and a small fire burning where the fireplace had been, he grabbed the rafters nearest them and heaved but even his enormous strength was useless against the crushing weight and realising Mike and the little boy where trapped below it, he shouted angrily, 'No, No No!'

Outside, the Mines Rescue Team reached the three women waiting anxiously outside, Aggie grabbing the first one saying, 'Tha's a bairn trapped inside there and the laddie that went in to get him hasn't come oot!'

The Team Leader walked calmly to the door to assess the situation as George Holland burst out and recognising the men, said, 'Thank God, ye ganna need jacks and props, it looks as if the ceiling and some of the roof has fallen in on them and tha's a fire building so you need to hurry.'

A member of the team was sent back to bring the Rescue vehicles closer just as the first ambulance arrived, parking up in the Fifth Row where two newly arrived policemen were trying to bring some order to the chaos of arriving emergency services. The first fire engine pulled up behind the Mines Rescue vehicles in the Sixth Row, the crew quickly dismounting to begin tackling the roaring fire in the coal trucks as another fire engine stopped in the Fifth Row parallel with the collapsed buildings in the Sixth. Quickly assessing the situation, the crew of the second fire engine knocked down a wall between coal houses and ran two hoses through and across the Sixth Row gardens to fight the smouldering fires in the collapsed houses as one of the Mine Rescue Team directed a fireman to try and douse the flames in the Turnbull's wrecked house.

A Fire Officer and Police Inspector walked round from the Fifth Row and approached the group standing next to the Mine Recue Trucks, the Inspector asking, 'Are you residents?'

Aggie and George Holland nodded.

The Fire Officer asked, 'Do you live in the Row?'

'Yes we dee,' Aggie replied brusquely.

Gesturing to the destroyed houses the Police Inspector asked, 'Good, do you know if any if these houses were occupied?'

Aggie answered impatiently, 'In a minute man, tha's a bairn and a lad trapped in the end hoose!'

'We know; the Mine Rescue Team is just about to go in, now what about these other houses?'

Rubbing her face irritably Aggie replied, 'Tha's nee one in Fifty One, tha at the Air Show, Mrs Rutherford is - was in Fifty Two, her husband will be at his allotment,' then stopping to hold back her tears, she continued, 'the Williamsons and their bairn were in number Fifty Three, I saw them not ten minutes before; Mrs Grundy was in but Aah divvint kna aboot the Strakers in Fifty Five.'

The Inspector took notes as George Holland Added, 'The Reagans in number Fifty Six are in a bit of a state but look okay, my Missus has taken them doon to wor hoose and the Thompsons in Fifty Seven are at the air show, that's everybody Aah think.'

The noise of the crash had brought shopkeepers and shoppers out onto the pavement when Tommy and the two Grundy lads ran into High Market and along to Kirkup's Bakery. Seeing the boys running toward her, Jane immediately feared the worse and hurried up to them asking, 'What's happened?'

Breathless and shocked, Tommy almost shouted, 'Crashed – a jet has crashed inte the Sixth Row, tha's fire's all ower.'

'The Ra's all knocked doon man,' Billy added as seven year old Roger wiped his nose and began crying loudly.

Horrified at what she was hearing and judging by the huge column of black smoke that was drifting over the Rows toward Ashington town centre, Jane new immediately that the boy's story was true.

Her heart beating madly she was almost afraid to speak but managed to ask, 'What about Mike, did you see him, is he alright?'

Billy wrapped his arm protectively around his sobbing brother as Ian replied, 'Aye Mam, he's alright, he sent us here,' and nodding at Billy and Roger, added, 'but Aah think their hoose has been smashed doon!'

Jane took a deep breath and said with a calmness she wasn't feeling, 'Right boys, I want you to go with Tommy to our house and stay there, I'm going round to fetch Mike, now remember, stay indoors.'

Handing her door keys to Tommy, she hurried along High Market as the first ambulances and police cars had raced by

A young Policeman positioned in the cut between the two end terraces of the Fifth Row was stopping folk from going to the crash site and despite pleading with him that her son was there, it was a good ten minutes before she managed to dodge round him and make her way to the corner of the gardens of the Sixth Row. What she saw stopped her in her tracks; the top half of the end house appeared to be slowly falling in on its self while all that remained of the next four houses was smouldering rubble that fire fighters were dousing with water while more men dug frantically into the rubble!

Walking down toward the rescue vehicles, she walked past an ambulance where in the back; she saw Alice Turnbull with her baby in her arms as an ambulance man tended one of her toddlers.

Seeing Aggie and George Holland standing outside the ruin that was number Fifty she hurried forward asking, 'Aggie have you seen my Mike?'

Clasping her hand to her mouth and unable to speak, Aggie could only nod as George placed his large dirty hand on Jane's shoulder, saying solemnly, 'He's in there lass, he pulled oot one bairn and went back in for the other, the Rescue Team are in there now using jacks to lift the floor to get te them!'

Shaking her head in disbelief, Jane felt her knees go weak and her stomach somersault, 'This could not be happening, not to one of her boys, not again,' she thought before saying, 'No that can't be, Tommy said he was alright! I've got to go to him.'

Still unable to speak, Aggie hugged Jane protectively and held her back, George saying, 'Yor lad's a bloody hero lass,' and pointing at another two men of the Mines Rescue Team carrying more equipment inside, he added, 'these lads will get him and the bairn oot, Pet.'

In the remains of Number 51, two firemen fought to free the body of Hugh Harley from the twisted and smashed remains of the cockpit of the Meteor while three more, aided by Albert, Arthur Galloway and Brian Compton, heaved a large section of aircraft frame from the debris of the Grundy's house. Throwing aside the twisted silver metal that bore an RAF roundel, the men stepped back to look carefully at where it had been.

Near collapse, his hands and arms bleeding and burnt, Albert leant on Arthur as one of the fireman lifted a large piece of rafter to one side before kneeling down, 'There's something here, something's moving,' he said.

Pedalling furiously in order to beat the traffic leaving the Air Show, the Hacky Dortys were just leaving Red Row when Ian suddenly braked to a halt causing the others to swerve round him as they too braked, wondering what was happening.
'Look.' He said, pointing south toward Ashington, 'look at all that smoke!'
Looking to where he was pointing, Howard said incredulously, 'Blidy hell that must be where the plane crashed!'
'Aye,' Ian said, 'but look where it is, that looks like it must be in Ashington somewhere.' The lads set off again, speculating wildly as to where the jet may have crashed, as Edward drove by tooting his horn and waving.

Arthur held Albert back as two firemen slowly and carefully moved debris creating a hole that one of them put his un-gloved hand through, saying quietly to the other, 'I can feel hair!'
Barely hearing what he had said, Albert asked excitedly, 'Is that Flo, is she moving, come on we've got to get her out man.'
The kneeling firemen lifted more debris away revealing a mound of black hair that suddenly moved. They recoiled as the shape wriggled and morphed into Monty the Grundy's dog who scrabbled from where he had been trapped and shaking itself, it created a small cloud of dust and then let out a pitiful howl before scampering off across the debris!
This was too much for Albert, he collapsed onto his knees sobbing as one of the fireman leaned into space where the Monty had lain

trapped. Gently brushing dust and debris from Flo Grundy's face, he shook his head sadly as he looked into her dead eyes!

The team of men worked quickly and efficiently in Number Fifty; with practiced skill they used jacks to lift the floor inch by inch, chocking it securely as they moved steadily forward, eventually reaching the crouched, lifeless and bloodied figure of Mike.

A police car parked in the middle of the junction in Ellington Village had sealed of the road to Ashington as Edward approached in his Sunbeam to join a growing queue of vehicles. Eventually stopping next to the policeman diverting traffic through Lynemouth or back through Longhirst, he asked why the road was closed.

Leaning down, the young policeman replied, 'An aeroplane has crashed on the edge of Ashington and we have had to close the road to allow the emergency services unhindered access, now please drive on sir.'

Shocked, Edward asked, 'Where has it crashed, do you know where?'

Waving them on, the policeman said, 'It hit the Rec Bridge and crashed into the Sixth Row, now keep moving.'

Sitting in the back of the car, Alice Thompson cried, 'Oh my God, Aah hope no one's hurt!'

Her husband Harry shook his head and added, 'It doesn't soond ower good does it?'

Driving past Ellington Colliery to follow the diversion through Lynemouth, Edward said, 'Right, Aah'll drop ye off at my house Mam then Dad and me will walk round and see what's happened, I doubt if we will be able to drive round there.'

When Albert saw the fireman shake his head he knew instinctively that Flo was gone and wearily rising to his feet as Arthur steadied him, he stumbled out of the rubble and into the street, the pain in his hands intensifying by the second as Arthur led him to an ambulance. Behind him the firemen worked quietly to recover Flo's battered and lifeless body while a few yards away the remains of Hugh Harley were gently laid on a stretcher.

Bent over, under the jacked up fallen roof, Tom Brodie the lead man in the rescue team, gently pulled a bloody and lifeless Mike back, revealing two year old Raymond who had been curled up below him, sobbing quietly. Tom reached past Mike and carefully lifted the filthy and blood drenched toddler out, passing him back to another member of the team behind him who passed the boy onto the Team Leader who cradling him gently, worked his way back outside.

Jane rushed forward and gasped in shock when she saw little Raymond who was covered in so much dirt and blood he was barely recognisable, 'Oh my God,' she gasped, 'how badly hurt is he?'

Handing the boy over to a waiting ambulance crewman, the Team Leader replied, 'He's got a broken arm but other than that, I think that he is okay.'

Shaking her head in disbelief, Jane asked, 'What about all that blood?'

Turning to go back inside, the Team Leader answered solemnly, 'It's not his blood!'

Jane grabbed his arm and asked desperately, 'What about my son, is it his blood, how badly hurt is he?'

Unable to look her in the eyes, he replied, 'We are bringing him out next, we'll have him out in a few minutes,' and hurried back inside.

Weaving in and out of cars queuing on the road into Ellington, the Hacky Dortys could see that the column of black smoke over Ashington had been reduced to wisps of grey smoke trailing across the still blue sky.

Reaching the road block, Ian asked the harassed policeman, 'Why hev ye blocked the Ashington Road?'

Waving traffic on he replied, 'The plane for Acklington crashed in the Sixth Row, now move on!'

His words hit the boys like a thunderbolt, 'But we live there,' shouted Howard.

His demeanour changing, the Policeman said, 'Am sorry lads, that's all I know, ye'll have to bike round by……' Before he could finish the five lads had pushed off past the police car and were pedalling furiously down Ellington bank on the closed road to Ashington.

It took Tom Brodie several minutes to cautiously move Mike into a position where he could pull him clear of where he had been trapped. Wrapping a large padded dressing around Mike's head, and preparing to move him out, he said to the rest of the team, 'He has a bad wound to the back of his head, a lot other cuts, two bad ones on his thigh and I think his left wrist is broken, I haven't managed to feel a pulse yet but I think he might still be alive!'

Running forward, Jane barely recognised the filthy blood stained figure that the team brought out on a collapsible stretcher, the Team Leader saying, 'He's alive Mrs but we need te get him into the ambulance and away te hospital noo!'

Tears running down her face, she turned to the ever dependable Aggie, and asked, 'Aggie can you call in and see the boys at my house, I left them on their own?'

Having seen the condition Mike was in, Aggie nodded through her own tears and replied, 'Aye Jane Pet, now go on we will look after the boys.'

By the time that the RAF Rescue Team arrived from Acklington, the Fire Brigade had all but extinguished the fires in the shunting yard and outhouses of the second terrace and the police had set up a Control Point a couple of hundred yards away in Bothal School Hall. A couple of the dinner ladies were called in and began to brew urns of tea and make sandwiches; it was going to be long night. Reporters and press photographers from regional newspapers were also beginning to arrive and began prowling round looking for a story and suitably dramatic photographs.

Jack Rutherford had rushed back from his allotment and had stood crying in the garden of Number 52 when the Firemen recovered his wife's body an hour after the crash. It would be another four hours before the bodies of the Eric and Barbara Williamson and three year old Alec would be recovered from Number 53.

Sweating and exhausted from their frantic bike ride, the Hacky Dortys raced past several police cars parked on either side of the level crossing before turning down the short dirt track to the end of the Sixth Row, abandoning their bikes to run into the rubble strewn street that was now full of men from the emergency services. They stopped to take in the scene, all of them gasping comments of shock and astonishment, all that is apart from Jake. He slowly walked down the Row to where his house had been and stood silently starring, unable to comprehend the scale of the disaster as tears began to roll down his cheeks.

Howard rushed into his house just as the police were asking everyone to leave their houses and go to Bothal School Hall. His mother, who had been talking to a still shocked Mr and Mrs Reagan, took hold of her son's arm, saying, 'Are ye alright Pet, you look lathered?'

Howard nodded and said unnecessarily, 'Haf the Row's gone Mam!'

'Aye Pet, noo I want ye to go with wor Mary roond to Bothal School and wait there, we'll be alang in a minute.

Ian, Rafe and Roger had looked in horror at the scene before walking to join Jake but they were stopped by a policeman, 'Ye cannit come doon here lads, it's too dangerous, noo if you've got relatives living here, ye need to go te Bothal School te find out aboot them!'

Rafe and Roger turned and walked back to their bikes but ignoring the policeman, Ian walked on toward the forlorn figure of his pal Jake standing crying in the street. George Holland stopped him saying, 'Ian lad, we need to get Jake to yor hoose, Billy and Roger are there with yor Tommy.'

Ian looked up at him and asked, 'What about Mr and Mrs Grundy?'

George shook his head and said quietly, 'Albert has been taken to hospital, his hands and arms are burnt but he's okay but am sorry to say that Mrs Grundy is dead.'

Ian sighed as George continued, 'Look son you have to know that your Mike is in hospital as well, he got trapped when he was rescuing the Turnbull bairns.'

Ian interrupted, 'Is he alright?'

'Whey, yer Mam's with him and he's alive, Aggie has gone ower to your hoose and I think ye should go there.'

Ian nodded and continued down the Row just as a black shape ran out of Albert's shed and began jumping up at a crying Jake who was too grief stricken to notice. Ian quietly walked up behind his pal and said, 'Jake; Billy and Roger are at my house and your Dad has burnt his hands and gone to hospital, you've got to come home with me, we can phone your Ronnie from there.'

Jake turned slowly, patted Monty and looking at Ian with tear filled eyes, said, 'Me Mam's dead isn't she?'

Tommy rushed to the door when Rafe and Ian led a still tearful Jake and subdued Monty into Hotspur House, asking Ian, 'Where's Mam and Mike?'

Guiding Jake into the sitting room he replied, 'Mam's at hospital with Mike, he's been hurt, come with Rafe and me to the kitchen, Billy and Roger need to be with Jake noo.'

As Aggie made tea for everyone, Billy and Roger joined Jake in the sitting room; Billy seeing the look on his older brother's face, asked, 'What's happened Jake, Aggie says Dad's in hospital and we won't be going back hyem?

Jake wiped his eyes and taking a deep breath, he waited until his two younger brothers sat down before saying, 'Look we won't be ganning back te the Sixth Ra, wor hoose has gone; Dad's in hospital, so we'll have to wait te speak to wor Ronnie te see what's ganning to happen.'

Roger sniffed hard and asked, 'But where's me Mam, she should be here man.'

A year older than Roger, Billy instantly realised from the look on Jake's face that their Mam would not be joining them and wrapping his arm protectively around Roger, he said quietly, 'Mam winnit be coming here Roger, she's gone te join Jesus!'

Rafe looked up the number for the Ship Hotel and after speaking for some time told Ian, 'Ronnie and his wife are out in their car so I have asked them to tell him to go straight to Ashington Hospital to see his father and that Jake and the other two are here.'

Ian said, 'Okay, Aggie is making some tea, I'll phone Maureen and Mike's girlfriend Jennifer and tell them what's happened.'

Sitting in the ambulance as it raced to Ashington Hospital, Jane watched with tears running down her face as the ambulance attendant placed an oxygen mask on Mike before wrapping a large dressing round the cut on his thigh in an effort to try and stop the bleeding.

Jane said quietly and hopefully, 'The bleeding means he is still alive!'

The attendant looked at her, nodded slightly and returned to work on Mike.

Having known of the crash for over an hour, the hospital was on full alert for casualties and within a minute of arriving a team of doctors and nurses were working on Mike as Jane watched, barely able to breathe.

Two hours later, as word spread of Mike's heroic actions and reporters tried to gain access to him, Jane with a tearful Jennifer standing behind her, sat beside his bed holding his right hand and talking gently to him. The wounds to the back of Mike's head and thigh had been stitched and dressed as had several other cuts on his arms and back. His broken left wrist was in a plaster and his right shoulder and upper back had been treated for first degree burns along with a second degree burn on his right forearm. Blood was slowly being dripped back inside him to make up for the three or more pints he had lost that had led to him losing consciousness.

When he had regained conscious, his first words had been, 'Is little Raymond alright?'

Albert Grundy's hands and forearms were severely burned and would take considerable care and treatment to prevent excessive permanent damage. Grief stricken at the loss of his mother, Ronnie had made it to his father's hospital bed just after six o'clock, leaving an hour later to be with his brothers and Mary in Jane's sitting room where many more tears were quietly shed.

Carrying five year old Elizabeth with his three other children trotting behind, Geordie Turnbull arrived at Ashington Hospital dreading what he was going to find. Hearing rumours of an aeroplane crashing in the 'Ra's he had caught the next bus from Newbiggin back to Ashington. Arriving just after four and with mounting panic he had tried to reach the Sixth Row but had been directed to Bothal School where he was told the full scale of the disaster and of the heroic rescue of his two children. The police drove him to the Hospital while Social Services arranged temporary accommodation for the family.

He found Alice sitting in the waiting room nursing baby Rosalind with Robert sitting next to her with his head resting on her arm.

Seeing her husband with her other children, Alice began to cry, saying, 'Eeee George hinny we've lost iviry thing, Aah even had to borrow nappies off the hospital!'

Sitting down next to her as the older children surrounded their mother, George asked, 'Where's Raymond, is he alright?'

'The poor mite has a broken arm and he's on a drip cos he's dehydrated but the doctor said he's ganna be alright.'

George smiled reassuringly at his wife and said, 'In that case we've lost nowt Pet, we hev iviry thing here, you and the bairns are alreet and that's all that matters at the minute.'

After helping his father secure his home in the Sixth Row, Edward dropped him off at his own house in Wansbeck Road and drove around to High Market where he spent the evening lending support, including collecting Jane from hospital at nine as Doctor Metcalf arrived to pick up Jennifer. Once home, Jane along with Mary and Aggie, began to organise the families. Social Services had called to say they were making arrangements for the Grundy children to be placed in foster homes until their father was well but Jane was having none of that.

'They will stay here with me until he is able to take care of them, I will not allow the boys to be split up,' she told them.

Roger and Billy were to have Mike's room for the time being and a foldaway bed was produced for Jake and put up in Ian and Rafe's room. Maureen, who had arrived with Terry earlier, reminded her mother that she had a spare bedroom if another one was needed.

Arthur Galloway collected Aggie later in the evening and told her that they were staying at his sister's in Portia Street until they were allowed back into the Sixth Row.

By midnight, as the RAF made plans to recover the remains of their aircraft the following day, only one fire engine and one police car remained at the crash site. Flight Lieutenant Mark Renshaw had faced some heavy grilling on his return to Acklington, finally climbing into his bed at one o'clock in the morning, knowing with some certainty that he would face a Courts Martial!

Chapter Nine
Recovery

The following morning dawned cool but sunny with the Sixth Row cordoned off by the police as the RAF took over control of the crash site in order to carry out their air crash investigation and recover what was left of the Meteor. The Ashington Branch of the National Union of Mineworkers had alerted the National Coal Board and pressed them for immediate action, resulting in several glaziers and roofers working on the damaged houses in the second terrace of the Sixth Row as well as the ones in the Fifth and Cross Rows. The crash site was also surrounded by reporters, photographers and a BBC film crew, all vying to capture the grimmest image.

While Wendy Robson sobbed inconsolably in her bedroom at the death of her beloved Hugh; a sombre organised chaos reigned in Hotspur house as Jane and Mary fed the six lads and themselves. Ronnie and Mary had spent the night on the bed settee in the sitting room so that they could be there for Ronnie's three younger brothers. Roger still appeared to be dazed and a little lost and Mary spent an hour being comforting him in the sitting room while Monty lay quietly at their feet.

Over a pot of tea in the kitchen, Jane and Ronnie discussed the immediate future, Jane saying, 'The boys can stay here until your father is back on his feet and is rehoused.'

Ronnie smiled and replied, 'That's great Jane, I obviously divvint hev anywhere to put them up at the minute and Aah don't think an Army flat would be suitable.'

'I agree, and if they stay with me they will be together and will be able to go to school when they are ready. I'll see what underclothes Ian and Tommy can give the boys until I can go down the street tomorrow.'

Ronnie smiled wryly, 'If they are owt like Aah was at their age, they winnit hev any under clathes Mrs Trevelyan and if you don't mind, Aah would like to buy them some new clothes and stuff tomorrow, I'm also ganning to phone Catterick and tell them what's going on and that I need to organise me Mam's funeral.'

Patting his hand, Jane said, 'I think there will have to be an inquest before anyone can be buried Ronnie, so it could take a while.'

Nodding, he said, 'I hadn't thought of that, I will tell my dad that you are looking after the boys when I go inte see him later teday.'

In his capacity as NUM official, George Holland along with another official, called round just before lunch to discuss with Jane and Ronnie their plans for supporting the Grundys. He told them that the NCB was going to prepare an empty house in the Third Row for Albert and the boys. Being the same size and layout as their old one; it was thought it would best meet their needs as the boys could remain at Wansbeck and Bothal School. George also informed them that it would need a bit of redecoration but he would be asking the NUM for funds to help with that and, provide money to buy furniture and household goods that had been lost in the crash. He also hinted that they would be approaching the RAF for compensation!

Aggie who had come over to help make Sunday dinner had been eavesdropping and shouted from the kitchen, 'Aah'll help we the decoration, am canny at hinging wallpaper!'

Thinking of the children Mike had risked his life saving, Jane asked, 'What about the Turnbulls, what's happened to them?'

The NUM Official, a thin sallow faced man, said, 'Tha bairn's are all fine apart from the two year old that your lad saved, he's got a broken arm but he'll be champion, the family spent last night in a hostel and we are hoping to move them into a three bedroomed house in Ariel Street sometime next week.'

George added, 'The Strakers at Number Fifty Five are staying with relatives until the NCB can find a hoose for them and we're not sure if Number Fifty Six is ganning te be repaired so we divvint kna what's happening with them at the minute. Ronnie If ye can come to the NUM offices behind Station Road the morn, someone will meet ye there and take ye to speak with the NCB to help sort things oot.'

Edward arrived as George and the other man left and after asking if there was anything the family needed, he took Jane into the garden, 'Am not sure if this is the right time to tell you or not Pet but as well the papers being full of the crash, tha's a bit in them about the McArdles.'

Jane's shoulders sagged as she said, 'What have they been up to now, I had forgotten all about them?'

'Apparently, there was a fire and explosion in tha caravan, one of them, or at least the police think it's one of them, was inside but tha's no sign of the other, and tha car's missing. The Police are searching for that and the other brother in case he was responsible as they are treating it as murder.'

Jane gasped, *'Murder?'*

'Yes Lass, apparently his head was bashed in!'

She sighed and said, 'Well I cannot say that I am sad or upset, I am just glad that I don't have them to worry about with all this going on!'

Later; Jane, Ronnie, Mary and the boys sat down to a quiet Sunday lunch that ended when Roger suddenly began crying into his pudding, blurting, 'This is like me Mam's.'

Mary quietly took him from the dining room into the sitting room where she sat consoling him until he asked, 'What time are we ganning te see me Dad please?'

It was just after two o'clock when Ronnie and his brothers walked into the Royal Victoria Infirmary in Newcastle to see their father who had been transferred there that morning to have his burns treated.

Sitting up in his bed in Ashington Hospital looking like a war hero, Mike smiled when his Mother, accompanied by Ian, Tommy and Rafe walked in at visiting time, he nodded hello to the two boys; Ian and Tommy nodding back as Rafe said, 'You look as though you been in an awful battle Mike!'

As Jane bent over to kiss him on the cheek, Mike replied, 'That's exactly how Aah feel Rafe lad!'

Tommy touched Mike's hand and asked, 'Are ye alright Mike, ye've got a lot of bandages on?'

Touching the large bandage around his head, Mike replied, 'Am fine Tommy lad, just a bit sore that's all, am more annoyed that Aah missed the match this morning, they hevn't got a chance withoot me, eh?'

Looking at his brother admiringly, Ian said, 'Mr Holland said you wor a hero Mike; that ye ran straight in te the Turnbulls when it was collapsing and that you were nearly killed!'

Jane stepped forward and said, 'Enough boys, you can ask him about it when he comes home, he needs rest now.'

Leaning over to the bedside table, Mike picked up a business card and handed it to his mother, 'The nurse gave me that just before visiting

Mam and said that this man is from the Daily News and want's to interview me, what de ye think?'

Jane took the card and read the name aloud, 'Peter Mansfield, he's one of the few with integrity Mike, it was him who wrote the true story about your father and Edward in Normandy so I suppose if you want someone to write exactly what *you* have to say, he is probably the one to speak to.'

Grinning Mike said, 'Aah've already been interviewed by blokes from the Evening Chronicle and Newcastle Journal!' His smile faded as he then asked, 'How are the Grundy boys, I was told they had moved Mr Grundy this morning and Mr Turnbull was allowed in to thank me for saving Robert and Raymond, which was a bit embarrassing like!'

Jane bent over and kissed Mike, 'You *are* a hero Mike, you almost killed me with worry yesterday but you deserve his thanks, you were very brave. Roger is not taking the loss of his Mum very well but Billy seems to have accepted it and Ronnie is being very good, he and Mary are looking after his brothers although they are going to stay with us until their father is fit again. Jake is different though, he is obviously distraught at losing his mother but he just appears to have grown up all of a sudden, I could be wrong though.

Ian nodded, 'He is different Mam but that started last week, he's still funny but a different kind of funny if ye know what I mean?'

After a five hour drive from Dortmund to the Belgian Border and through the North West corner of France during the early hours of Monday morning, Bill Armstrong stopped on the car deck, pulled on the handbrake of his Triumph and switched off the engine. The smell of diesel, petrol, hot engines and the sea was over almost over powering when he climbed out, stretched his arms above his head and twisted from side to side, 'It might not have been such a good idea to buy a little sports car,' he thought before pulling on his tweed jacket and making his way up to the passenger deck of Calais to Dover Ferry. Walking into the cafeteria, he bought himself a pot of tea, a stale looking ham sandwich and a copy of this morning's Daily Express before sitting by one of the many windows to watch the ship sail slowly out of Calais.

Staring out of the window, he reflected on his weekend; it had been less than successful and almost a total wasted journey. As he had thought, it was Sunday before his ex-wife Irma reluctantly agreed to allow him to visit her and his son, albeit in her new home with her new husband present! The meeting had not gone well; Wilhelm almost hiding behind her, Irma had been hostile from the start, accusing Bill of trying to destroy the new life she was building for herself and her son.

When he had pointed out that the boy was his son too, Hannes, her new husband had walked over to him and began to berate him in German whilst wagging his finger in his face. This was too much for Bill; he had jumped up from his chair and towering over the German by at least eight inches; forced him to recoil backwards in fright and fall into his own chair where he sat looking visibly shaken.

It was what happened next that made Bill realise the futility of his visit; Wilhelm ran from behind his mother and wrapping his arms around Hannes' neck he had asked, 'Bis du OK Pappa?'

Shaking his head in resignation, Bill said, 'Well that just about sums the situation up,' then looking directly at his son, he said slowly, 'Wilhelm, wenn sie hilfe benötigen, vergessen Sie nicht, Ich bin dein Vater,' (Wihlem, if you are ever in trouble, never forget that I am your Father) then turned and walked out.

Finishing his sandwich, he took a sip of tea, picked up the paper and looked at the photograph and headline on the front page, gasping, 'My God!'

'Air Disaster in Northumberland'

It was the subtitle that shocked him;

'RAF Pilot blamed as Jet Fighter Crashes into the Coal-Mining Town of Ashington.'

He gasped again when he looked closely at the photo of the destroyed Sixth Row, recognising it despite the devastation. He read the front page and the next four pages that told the story of the disaster, the fatalities and of the dramatic rescue of the Turnbull children.

'Nick's family are certainly being put through the mill,' he thought as he flipped through the paper, stopping when his attention was grabbed by the word Ashington on a small heading on the sixth page;

'Caravan Explosion near Ashington in Northumberland - Police Suspect Murder'

Rubbing his chin he read of the death of one of the McArdles and the disappearance of the other and of the nationwide police search for the missing brother and their car.

Having read the article, he threw down the paper and walked off to the bar to buy himself a large whisky as he said quietly, 'Good bloody riddance to bad rubbish!'

The following day, back in Ashington, NCB housing representatives toured the crash site with their architect, surveyor and foreman builder to assess the damage and decide the future of the battered third terrace of the Sixth Row. The on-site meeting ended at the top of the Row out of earshot of the RAF team who were finishing their recovery of the destroyed aircraft.

The Housing Manager asked, 'So, we agree that we can repair and strengthen the dividing wall between Number Fifty Five and Number Fifty Six making that the new gable end of a much shortened Row and, that we will clear the remains of the destroyed six houses?'

The other's all nodded in agreement apart from the architect who asked, 'Why not rebuild all of the damaged houses?'

'Because all of the Second to Sixth Rows and Cross and Long Rows are due for demolishing in the foreseeable future, and please remember that information is not for general publication gents, especially to those that live here, got that?'

They all nodded and headed off toward the Colliery, the Housing Manger discussing the clearances and landscaping of the site with the Building Foreman.

'Cleared, levelled and turfed is the order I have received from on high to pass onto you Joe,' The Manager said.

In Green Lane, Wendy's mother ensured that her daughter did not see a newspaper or listen to the news on the radio or television that were full of the crash, most of them commenting that it was the recklessness of Hugh that had caused the accident. Wendy was beside herself with grief, her mother fearing that if she realised she was partly to blame for the tragedy, she would become suicidal. The press having not yet linked her to Hugh's low flying, her mother intended to drive her down to Essex where she would stay with her sister.

Not long after Tommy, Ian and Rafe had left for school, Ronnie arrived with Mary to collect his brothers and took them into town and spent some time in Shepherd's Store where Mary took charge of buying them enough shoes, clothes and underwear to last them at least twelve months.

Mary tried her best to be cheerful and positive but the boys went through the motions of trying on clothes without any real enthusiasm resulting in the very tall and jovial sales assistant remarking, 'Come on lads, cheer up, it's not the end of the world, yer only trying clothes on!'

Mary grabbed his arm and dragging him to one side, scolded him before explaining why the boys were so morose. The sight of the tall youth with his head lowered like a naughty child as diminutive Mary berated him did put a grin on Jake's face.

Looking at his brother, he said, 'She's nee softie is she Ronnie?'

'She's been through some bad times Jake, so she's a lot tougher than she looks.'

It was two o'clock before Peter Mansfield accompanied by a photographer, managed to interview Mike, 'Hello Michael, at last I get to meet the Hero of the air-crash,' he said as he pulled up a chair next to Mike's bed.

'I'm no hero, Aah only did what anybody would dee man.'

Peter shook his head, 'No not many people would run into a burning, collapsing building and crawl into such a tiny space, not once but twice, that takes a special sort of man. I have spoken to Mr Holland and he has told me just how terrifying it must have been crawling into that tiny, dreadful space.'

'Whey, I had to be rescued myself didn't I, if I am a hero, then so are the men that rescued me.'

'Yes they are Mike but they are trained for that and they had special equipment to help them and keep them safe, it is their job but you were superb, the Rescue Team told me that you were crouched over the boy, shielding him from, falling bricks as well as the fire, that's the action of a hero Michael.'

Blushing, Mike replied, 'I never thought about it man, when Mrs Turnbull told me her boys were missing, Aah just went into get them out, I was the only one there at the time so I had too didn't I?'

'There are many that wouldn't have gone in and very few would have crawled into the collapsing building Michael and anyway, Mrs Galloway has said that you also saved Mr Grundy's life?'

Puzzled, Mike answered, 'No man, I just pushed him out the road of the plane, that's all.'

'Come on now, Mrs Galloway said you dived six foot, knocking Mr Grundy into his brick shed, if you had not have done that you both would have been badly injured or worse, look what happened to your motorbike.'

'Aye, the last I saw of that it was smashed and burning, I don't suppose anybody rescued that for me?'

Beginning to write short hand notes in his pocket book, Peter replied, 'I don't suppose they have Michael but I wouldn't worry about that as I'm sure that your story will earn you at least a replacement motorbike from my newspaper!'

Peter asked Mike to describe the crash and the rescues and his thoughts during and after. He also asked him about his family, girlfriend and his football team before standing back to allow the photographer to take several photos of the injured hero.

Sitting back down, he said, 'You now that I covered the sad story of your father Michael, it has been good to cover this one about a true hero from your street but I have also been told that you helped rescue your younger brother earlier this year?'

'Wor Ian was the hero then man, he held Tommy up for hours in that freezing marsh, all I did was run in and help pull them out.'

Peter stood up and shaking Mike's hand said, 'Thanks for talking to me Mike, you are a true, instinctive and modest hero and I am sure people are going to be talking about your bravery for a long time, they are already talking about an award.'

Lying in his hospital bed with his fore-arms and hands propped inside two raised covers, Albert Grundy forced a smile when his three very smartly dressed youngest boys walked into the ward to see him at visiting time.

Trying to be cheerful for them he said, 'Whey ye buggers! Look at ye three toffs, hev ye got aall dressed up just te come and see me?'

Ronnie and Mary shepherded the boys closer to their father where Billy and Roger being not sure what to say, stood in awkward silence leaving to Jake to explain, 'Ronnie and Mary took wi shopping for clathes Dad cos we had nowt to left to wear after the crash.'

Holding back the tears that were welling up in his eyes, Albert said, 'Thanks Ronnie, I'm sorry am in here when Aah shud be oot there sorting things oot.'

Ronnie explained that Jane was looking after the boys and that he needn't worry as the NCB had already found them an empty house and that it would be furnished and ready for him when he left hospital. Albert explained he did not know exactly how long he would have to remain in hospital but a nurse had suggested to him that it could be several weeks.'

Sighing as he remembered, he asked, 'What aboot Monty is he alreet?'

Jake replied, 'He's alright Dad, he's with us at Mrs Trevlan's.'

Then Albert embarrassed them all while making them giggle, 'Ye kna the worst is, Aah cannit wipe me an bum or tek a blidy piddle mesell, man that's not right is it!'

The lads avoided talking of the loss of their mother, none of them yet able to mention her without becoming tearful and when their father said, 'Be good lads and behave for Mrs Trevelyan, divvint let yor Mam doon noo,' Roger began to sob and once again had to consoled by Mary.

Much to everyone's surprise, the following morning Jake decided he wanted to do his paper round and go back to school, persuading Billy and Roger that they should also go back to school. Jane thought it was a good idea and said she would walk to school with them and Tommy.

Completing his paper round by half past seven, Jake burst in through the kitchen door clutching a newspaper, 'Look at this,' he said holding it up to show Jane and the others, 'it's Mike, tha's pictures of him and a story, look at the headlines man!'

'Teenage Hero of Air Crash'

Jane took the newspaper from Jake, looked at the large photo of a bandaged Mike smiling from his hospital bed and said, 'Doesn't he look handsome,' and then read the first few paragraphs aloud before saying, 'Come on school, we'll read it all later.'

Later that morning, Detective Chief Inspector Fairbanks handed the McArdle case over to Detective Sergeant Jamie Norman. The two of them had spent the last two days going over the facts they had compiled, which were;

The McArdles were last seen when they left the Grand Hotel at eleven o'clock on Friday.

The fire and explosions were reported at twelve thirty by the farmer on whose land the caravan sat.

Only one badly burnt and unrecognisable body was found in what was left of the caravan.

The pathologist report shows the likely cause of death was one of several blows to the head.

Due to the extreme damage, the Fire Brigade are unable to determine the cause of the fire that led to the whisky bottles igniting and the gas cylinders exploding.

There is no trace of the other brother or their car despite a nationwide police alert.

There was no usable forensic evidence from the remains of the caravan or the area outside that had been churned into a quagmire by fire fighters.

DCI Fairbanks handed over the file and said to DS Norman, 'What you've told me of the McArdles and their lifestyle and what we have subsequently found out about them would lead anyone to the only and obvious conclusion that the two brothers had a drunken argument ending with one killing the other and then fleeing. Well that all seems far too neat to me so we have to hope that someone spots him or he turns up somewhere. In the meantime I want you to keep digging and see what else you can come up with. Either way, I'll leave it with you, oh and let me know if and when they identify which McArdle was in the caravan.'

Jamie nodded and replied, 'Okay Sir, I still think the one that is on the run is probably heading back to Ireland, hopefully he might be caught trying to get over there if he is still in the car.'

'I wouldn't bank on that Sergeant; he can't be that stupid, can he?'

Jamie shook his head but smiled wryly before saying, 'I'm going to speak to Mrs Trevelyan later to find out when she last saw them.'

'Why do you want to speak to her, do you think that she can shed more light on the matter?'

'I'm just trying to nail down their last few days to see if there had been any signs of friction between the brothers, that's all Sir.'

Giving Jamie a quizzical look, the DCI warned, 'Yes okay but make sure you are not just visiting her because she's a stunner!'

That was exactly why he wanted to speak to Jane and he did so just before lunch when he called on her at the Bakery. She took him down to Hotspur House where they talked about the last time she had seen the McArdles and their visit to Maureen. Eventually Jane said, well if that's all Sergeant, sorry Jamie, I have lunch to prepare for the boys and Mr Thomson.'

'Edward Thomson is coming here?'

'Yes he is helping out as he always does.'

Looking annoyed, he thanked her and saying cheerio left, walking down the path and straight into Edward who had just parked his Commer van.

Jamie stopped him, 'Ah Mr Thompson, can I have a quick word please?'

Edward nodded and replied, 'Aye of course Sergeant,' and walked back to stand alongside his van as Jamie followed.

'You've obviously heard about the McArdles?'

Sensing some hostility in the Sergeant's words, Edward replied, 'Yes, I've read the papers.'

'I recall that you had a bit of a scuffle with them last week is that correct?'

'Yes, you are well aware I did, they had threatened Mrs Trevelyan's daughter and I went to have a word with them and they became aggressive and yes, we exchanged blows, why?'

Jamie did not answer and instead asked, 'Mr Thompson where were you last Friday night around midnight?'

'In me bed asleep on my own, why, where were you?'

Ignoring the question, Jamie continued, 'So you have no one who can confirm that?'

'I've just said I was alone so of course I haven't, why?'

Frowning, Jamie said, 'Well you had a fight with the McArdles, I'm just wondering what your feelings were toward them?'

Controlling his mounting anger, Edward replied in a calm and measured tone, 'I have no love for the McArdles, they were cowardly bullies and criminals that your lot should have locked up a long time ago and I can't say I'm not happy about what has happened but as far as I was concerned our disagreement had been resolved, now what about you, you had a couple of run ins with them didn't you?

Jamie stepped back and said, 'I have yet to convince my DCI that they had a drunken argument that resulted in one of them being killed by the other who then set fire to their caravan before fleeing; so until we track him down and convict him, or some other new evidence comes to light I have to keep making enquiries.'

Edward smiled sardonically and said, 'So you haven't managed to convince your DCI yet eh! You still haven't said where you were that night,' and turning he walked up the drive to Jane's kitchen door.

It was after nine o'clock before Bill wearily parked his car behind his mother's house in Newbiggin; it had been a tiring few days and he was exhausted when he slumped into the chair in front of the sitting room fire as his mother cooked him sausage and eggs.

His Aunty Margaret brought him a cup of tea and said, 'There's been a right carry on around here while you've been away Bill.'

Taking the tea gratefully, he responded, 'If you're talking about the aeroplane crashing into your old street and the McArdles, I read about in the paper this morning; that was a right blidy carry on eh?'

A little later as he sat in the kitchen eating the food, he told the sisters of his wasted trip and how different his son appeared, closing the matter with, 'I don't think there's much chance of me seeing him again, at least not until he's old enough to think for himself without her brainwashing him.'

Pouring himself a whisky from the duty free bottle he had brought back with him he sat down again and said, 'Come on then, tell me all there is to know about the crash and those buggas the McArdles.'

On the Wednesday after the crash, the families were allowed to move back into the top end of the Sixth Row as the builders began repairing the wall that was to become the new gable end while a small crane with a grab began clearing the rubble from the destroyed houses into a waiting line of NCB trucks.

Chapter Ten
Moving On

Having collected Mike from hospital at eleven o'clock on Friday morning, Jane picked up the handset of the ringing telephone when she walked back into Hotspur House; Maureen's worried voice saying, 'Mam, I think the baby is on its way!'
Smiling at a puzzled Mike who was standing behind her in the hall, Jane replied, 'I'm on my way darling.'
 Four hours later, Amanda Jane Proudlock uttered her first hungry cry in the Maternity Ward of Ashington Hospital and after a quick clean-up, was handed over to her exhausted but beaming mother who cuddling her said, 'Eee, wait until your daddy sees you!'

Later that evening, after visiting hours at the Maternity Ward, there was a subdued party atmosphere in Hotspur House. Mike's return home and the birth of Maureen's baby were celebrated quietly by Trevelyans, Grundys and Proudlocks, mindful that the Grundy boys were still mourning the loss of their mother.

Early the following morning two cars left Newbiggin heading for Catterick, Ronnie and Mary were due to take over their Married Quarter at ten o'clock and Big Bill was going to book into the Sergeant's Mess and meet the RSM of the outgoing unit, the 1st Battalion of 'The Yorkshire Fusiliers'.

Although the two bedroomed mid terraced house was tiny and heated only by the coal fire in the sitting room of their new married quarter, Mary was delighted to see that it had an upstairs bathroom and two portable 'Aladdin' heaters but what impressed her the most was the amount of household items that Ronnie checked as the Barrack Inventory Accountant (BIA) read out from his list. There was everything from beds and bedding to crockery and cutlery, all any small family needed for day to day living.

After the meters had been read and the BIA left, Mary asked, 'Is all this stuff ours now Ronnie?'

Grinning, he replied, 'No darling, we have a loan of it while we are living here and we have to pay for any losses or damages.'

Picking up a glass tumbler from the glass and crockery lined up on the table, she said, 'Then you better not break anything Pet!'

Laughing at her use of the Geordie term of endearment, he said, 'Yes Mary, now come on we have a lot of stuff to put away and a bed to make up.'

Smiling naughtily, she added, 'And to test Ronnie!'

The following morning, inspecting the new light brown tiled fireplace that the NCB installed in place of the old black-leaded kitchen range they had ripped out of the house allocated to the Grundy's in the Third Row, Aggie Galloway said to her husband Arthur, 'Eeee that looks champion but where on earth are they ganna cook?'

Pointing to a newly installed power point next to the pantry door, he replied, 'Whey it looks like tha ganna hev an electric cooker.'

Screwing her face in disgust, Aggie spat, 'Ye cannit cook a proper meal on one of them man, ye cannit beat the big owld ranges, what a shame!'

The two of them had arrived a few minutes earlier to wall paper the kitchen and sitting room and after a quick walk round began preparing the walls when their attention was grabbed by a tap at the back door followed by a woman's voice saying loudly, 'Aye, Aye, Aah saw ye's carrying the wallpaper in so Aah've come te give ye a hand, am Jen from next door,' and laughing so loud, that her three double chins wobbled, she said, ' iviry bugga caalls me Jolly Jen, Aah nah poor Albert and used te play Bingo we Flo at the 'Tute' so Aah'll be here te keep an eye on him and the bairns when they move in, noo where shall Aah start?'

Glaring at the huge pinnie wearing woman who was at least eight inches taller than her and with huge meaty arms that she almost managed to cross below her enormous bosoms; Aggie replied testily, 'We can manage thanks, we've got iviry thing sorted.'

Seeing the resentment in his wife's demeanour, Arthur stepped forward and said, 'Come on noo Aggie, we can dee we a hand, ye can start scrapping the owld wallpaper off in the sitting room, that'll leave us to crack on in here.'

Aggie gave her husband a crooked smile and went back to mixing wall paper paste as Jen shouted over her shoulder, 'Right ye lot, get yer arses in here tha's work te be done, get into the sitting room and get the wall paper of the waalls while Aah gan hyem and mek dinna!'

Arthur and Aggie watched in amazement as a small, thin, dour looking man led four very reluctant looking lads aged between eleven and sixteen through the kitchen and into the sitting room; the dour looking man saying quietly, 'Alreet Arthur,'

'Alreet Joe,' Arthur replied.

Leaving the bucket of paste, Aggie stepped across to Jen and looking up at her said, 'Aah'll be making sure things are done properly in here, Aah divvint want any shoddy work done for Albert and the bairns, their Ronnie's hoping te be back the morn or Tuesda te dee some painting.'

Recognising that Aggie may have thought that she was trying to upstage her, Jen replied, 'Aye of course Pet, just tell them buggas in there what te de and if ye hev any bother from them, give me a shout and

Aah'll fettle tha lazy arses for them. The big gowpy looking bugga in there is wor Bill; the daft sod left school last year and still hasn't got a job so he can dig ower the garden the morn. Aah leave ye te it and if ye want a cup of tea, just come next door and we'll have a natter while these buggas get on we the work.'

At eight o'clock the following morning Ronnie paraded with the Advance Party outside the 1930's Barrack block allocated to them in Haig Barracks. Big Bill watched from one side as Sergeant Major Tom Barclay called the roll and briefed the men on the tasks ahead of them. Immediately after the parade, Ronnie approached the Sergeant Major and asked if he could speak to the RSM.

Tom Barclay gave him a withering look and replied, 'That's a coincidence because he wants to see you Corporal, go on march over and report to him.'

Marching quickly over to where Bill was standing, Ronnie slammed to attention in front of him but before he could speak, Bill said, 'Relax Corporal, look I read in the papers the sad news that your mother was one of those killed in the plane crash.'

Ronnie nodded as Bill continued, 'I have spoken to Major Timison and told him about your mother and that your father is in hospital; he has granted you two weeks compassionate leave as I'm sure you will have a funeral to organise. What about your brothers? Who is looking after them while your father is in hospital?'

Ronnie explained how Jane had taken them in and about the NCB allocating the family another house and thanked Bill for arranging the two weeks leave.

Bill then asked, 'Corporal, I see you have a car and I have to ask how you can afford that?'

Ronnie smiled slightly, 'I got a dowry off my wife's brother Sir.'

'You did bloody well there lad, marrying a cracker like her and money as well, go on then, and make sure you phone camp if you have any problems.'

The first funerals of the air crash victims took place at a full and over-flowing Holy Sepulchre Church on the following Monday. The grief felt in the church when the tiny coffin of three year old Alec Williamson was placed alongside those of his mother and father's in front of the congregation was almost too much for the grieving relatives; the Vicar having to wait five long minutes before he began the service. Most of the folk from the 'Rows' were there as well as a representatives from RAF Acklington, the NCB and NUM. The National and local press were out in force but even they showed restraint throughout the morning and into the afternoon when Helen Rutherford's funeral took place with a similar congregation in St Aidan's Roman Catholic Church next to the Regal Cinema.

His arms still heavily bandaged, Albert Grundy was supported by Ronnie while Mary held the hands of Billy and Roger, with Jake walking alongside as they entered St Aidan's on Wednesday morning. The Church was again overflowing as family, friends and mining families from all over Ashington came to mourn the loss of Flo Grundy. After the burial, family and close friends walked or drove down to the Grand Hotel in the centre of town where Ronnie had arranged food and drinks in the upstairs function room.

The initially subdued atmosphere changed slowly as the room filled and sherry, beer and a few whiskies were drunk.

Ronnie helped Albert to a chair and asked, 'Can Aah get you a cup of tea Faather?'

Albert gave his son a hurt look, replying, 'Am not drinking tea to say goodbye to my Flo, get me a whisky lad.'

Smiling sadly, Ronnie asked, 'Are ye allowed alcohol Faather?'

'Aah divvint give a damn what am allowed, I'll hev a whisky.'

A couple of minutes later, Jake took the tumbler full of whisky that Ronnie and brought from the bar and held it to his father's lips. Albert took a sip, then using his bandaged hand to push Jake's hand and the tumbler up, he took a large gulp before saying, 'That's better, thanks Jake lad.'

Mary looked after Billy and Roger while a long line of friends and relatives slowly paid their condolences to Albert, Ronnie and Jake who, looking very smart in a new navy blue, Italian style suit stood dutifully by his father for most of the afternoon. His resolve to stay at his side was tested when Aggie Galloway trotted toward him and he realised what was going to happen!

Not able to escape, he managed to smile painfully as she grabbed him to her bosom saying, 'Eeeeee, yer Mam would be proud of ye teday if she could see ye Jake lad,' and planted her lips wetly on his cheek, holding them there while she hugged him for a few seconds that to him seemed to be much longer.

After Aggie had kissed and fussed over Albert, he turned to Jake who was still blushing after his close encounter with Aggie, and said, 'Jake lad, Aah think ye best tek a drink of that whisky yer howlding!'

Remembering what had happened when he had inadvertently drunk whisky at Maureen's wedding, Jake shook his head and replied, 'Nur thanks Dad.'

A little later, walking home through Ashington with Ian who had been given the day off school, Jake pointed to three Teddy Boys standing outside the café next to the Buffalo Cinema and said, 'A few weeks ago, I begged me Mam to buy me a suit like that and Aah telt her that Aah thowt they looked brilliant and tha were all the fashion. She telt me not te be blidy daft cos she cudn't afford it and even if she cud she wudn't cos the look sackless and that ye shud only buy things that divvint gan oot of fashion!' He sighed deeply and said quietly, 'She was alwas right like.'

The next day, lino and loose carpets were laid in the newly decorated house in the Third Row and in the afternoon as Edward Thomson wired in a new Electric cooker, Ronnie supervised Doggart's and Arrowsmith's delivery men as they carried in furniture and boxes of crockery, cutlery and pots and pans. Sorting out the pantry, Mary giggled at the antics of Aggie and Jolly Jen who had been trying to outdo each other all morning and now appeared to be engaged in a competition to see who could make up the most beds! She and Ronnie moved in that night and lit the fires in the sitting room and kitchen, bringing the house to life in readiness for Albert and the boys coming home, the following Monday.

While Mike was football training for the first time since the crash, Jane decided that she would try and give the rest of the Grundy boys a fun day before they moved into their new home. On Saturday morning, she and Edward drove Ian, Rafe, Jake, Tommy, Billy and Roger the dozen or so miles to the popular seaside resort of Whitley Bay, parking their cars close to the white painted Edwardian, Spanish City amusement park that overlooked the sea. The distinctive seventy five foot high dome over the renaissance-style frontage marked the entrance to the permanent fun fair, where within minutes the boys were whooping it up on the Waltzer before enjoying themselves on the other rides as Jane and Edward walked around the stalls.

The lads had a terrific time; the older ones ensuring that Billy and Roger were looked after, even on the Ghost train when the lads all tried to scare each other as they sat in the cars that clanked around the dark tunnels. After a lunch of fish and chips, they left the Spanish City and crossing the road, walked through the well-manicured gardens and on to the promenade.

When the boys charged down to the beach, Jane shouted, 'We'll meet you at the cars in an hour,' then linking Edward, the two of them walked along the promenade toward the sea front Rendezvous Café, enjoying the late summer sun and fresh breeze from the sea.

Sitting in the Café sipping 'Frothy Coffee', mindful that it had only been a few month's since her abusive and drunken husband had been hung for murder and afraid of ruining the moment, Edward put his hand on Jane's and said, 'It's been a grand day with the lads Jane but it would be nice if we could have a day on our own; when you're ready that is and if you would like to?'

Smiling, Jane replied, 'Yes please, how about next Saturday, Mike can look after Tommy in the afternoon; that is if he's not playing football.'

Grinning like the Cheshire Cat, Edward replied, 'He better not be!'

Sitting in the front seat of his son's car, Albert still had a light dressing on his left hand with a slightly larger one on his right when Ronnie pulled up outside the Grundy's new home in the Third Row. Mary and the boys were standing at the gate of the small yard, Jake stepping forward to open the door for his father as Jolly Jen, with an inane grin, stood at her gate next door watching him arrive.

A gentle drizzle had dampened the streets and the mood as Albert; not wanting to become emotional, nodded to Mary and the boys and walked into the centre of the kitchen and stopped to slowly look around.

Ronnie came up behind him, 'Everybody helped to get it ready for ye Dad and the NUM provided money for most of the furniture, Mary and me got the rest and Jane Trevelyan bought the pictures and mirrors.'

'Ye've aall done a grand job lad; yer Mam wud hev loved this eh?'

Seeing tears in her Father-in-Law's eyes, Mary took his arm and said, 'Please come and sit down Mr Grundy, we have tea ready and Mrs Trevelyan has sent lovely cakes from bakery for you.'

Allowing her to lead him to the large cosy armchair in front of the sitting room fire, Albert chided her gently, 'Look Mary Pet, ye cannit keep calling me Mr Grundy, please call me Albert or Dad!'

Handing him a cup of tea, Mary said, 'Yes Dad.'

War almost broke out at five o'clock!

Jolly Jen had just carried in a large metal pan filled with delicious smelling mince and dumplings and placed it benevolently on the kitchen table when Aggie trotted in with two corned beef and potato pies!

Standing with a pie in each hand, Aggie glared at the pan of mince and dumplings and demanded, 'Did ye mek that, ye must hev known, that Aah'd be bringing food te day!'

Giggling as she walked past the two women who were glaring defensively at each other, Mary opened the door of the new electric cooker releasing the delicious aroma of roast chicken and said, 'Look, I have cooked dinner as well!'

Having risen from his chair, Albert stood in the doorway to the sitting room and said, 'Whey ye buggas a Hell, we've enough blidy food to feed the street man!'

Jen began to chortle infectiously and placing her mighty arm around Aggie's shoulder she said, 'Whey Aggie Lass, we're ganna hev to get wor sells sorted oot or tha's ganna be a lot big fat buggas like me in here or else wa ganna waste a lot of blidy gud food Petal!

Aggie grinned and said, 'Aye we are, de ye want a plate pie?

Chapter Eleven
A Picnic to Remember

The Hacky Dortys cycled off to Newbiggin early on Saturday morning and a little later, Mike riding his new BSA motorbike took Tommy with him for a day out in Morpeth with Jennifer leaving Jane to prepare a picnic for Edward and her. Wearing a lemon tight fitting jumper with matching cardigan fastened at the neck over close fitting blue trousers, she was waiting by the door with the picnic basket and a tartan rug at ten o'clock when he pulled up outside Hotspur house. Hurrying down the path, she kissed him quickly on the lips and handed him the basket and rug before climbing into the front seat. Casually dressed in slacks and Jumper, he stowed the picnic in the boot and climbed into the driver's seat before driving off north to the historic sandstone town of Alnwick where he joined the A1 and continued north as they chatted none-stop.

Connected by a causeway that is covered twice a day by the tide, Lindisfarne or Holy Island lies a mile off the north Northumberland mainland. Driving slowly across the still damp causeway and onto the beach of the island toward the quaint village that is dominated by the stunning ruins of Lindisfarne Priory, Edward parked in the centre of the village and the two of them set off to explore the Priory and a little later, the castle that stood atop a rocky outcrop overlooking a small bay that contained a small fleet of fishing cobles swaying in a gentle swell.

Jane looked radiant and happier than Edward had ever seen her as they strolled hand in hand back to the car to collect the picnic and the tartan rug. Walking back out past the castle to the dunes at castle Point, they found a sheltered spot looking down the mainland to the mighty

Bamburgh Castle a few miles south. After enjoying the picnic and finishing the bottle of white wine she had packed, Jane lay back on the sand, smiling up at Edward. He leaned over and kissed her tenderly and felt her wrap her arms around his shoulders, pulling him back for a longer and more passionate kiss, the kiss he had dreamed of for so long. He could feel both their hearts beating and struggled to hold back, still afraid to rush; still afraid that he would misread the situation.

After several more passionate kisses, Jane asked, 'What time is it Edward?'

Thinking he had ruined it, he looked at his watch and replied, 'It's after three,' then looking at the sea, added, 'the tides on its' way in, I suppose we better head back to the car before it's too late to get off the Island.'

Jane smiled up at him and said, 'I think it's already far too late Edward!'

'No, we still have plenty of,' but he stopped when he saw her smiling at him and instead said, 'yes I think we might be too late, it does come in very fast.'

Later, having telephoned home to tell Mike that they had been stranded by the tide, they walked into the olde world Manor House Hotel that had been the home of the local lords of several Manors; Jane linking Edward as he asked the woman at reception, 'Have you a room for the night, we've been caught out by the tide.'

The woman smiled knowingly and replied, 'Yes it happens all the time; we have a double room with lovely views of the castle or a twin at the front?'

Edward looked at Jane quizzically and she smiled and said, 'Oh the double don't you think darling, we must have the view!'

The front door of Hotspur House remained open all through the evening of the following Saturday as family and friends arrived to help Jane and Edward celebrate their engagement. The celebration came as a welcome relief after a difficult and tragic few months but at long last Jane could look to the future without dread, happy that the man she loved would be by her side.

The house was full of laughter and chatter as more and more folk arrived, all wanting to congratulate the couple on what most of them had always thought was inevitable. Aggie scuttled round like a contented mother hen, smiling at everyone and kissing anyone too slow to escape her clutches. A gaggle of men stood in the garden, drinking beer and smoking cigarettes and putting the world to right while inside Jane was happy to show her engagement ring to anyone who asked. Edward kept looking across at her, hardly able to believe that they were at long last, a couple.

The Hacky Dortys had arrived early and filled their bellies from the copious amounts of food laid on out on the dining room table before leaving the 'Grown Ups Party' to go off to the flicks!

A few minutes later, Doctor Jonathon Metcalf arrived with his daughter Jennifer and blonde-haired Sandra Phillips who Edward had taken to the Ball.

As Jennifer rushed over to Mike and Sandra said hello to Jane, Jonathon asked Edward, 'I hope you don't mind me bringing Sandra but we are a bit of an item now.'

Grinning, Edward replied, 'No that's champion Jonathon, she is a bonny lass and I can see yer both happy.'

'That we are old man,' he replied.

Before Mike and Jennifer left the party to go to the Arcade dance, Jonathon spoke to him in the hall, 'I'm glad to see you have fully recovered Mike, no lasting damage I hope?'

'No I'm fit, back at work and playing football again thanks.'

Placing his hand on Mike's shoulder, he said, 'Mike I have to tell you that I admire you tremendously, what you did took enormous courage. You fully deserve your George Cross; do you know when the investiture is?'

Blushing, Mike replied, 'I'm still waiting to be told but it's a bit embarrassing like.'

'Embarrassing! Not at all Mike, you deserve every plaudit aimed at you, you go along and enjoy the moment, it happens to only a few.

In Catterick, resplendent in their scarlet Mess uniforms, the Warrant Officers' and Sergeants' of The Kings Own Northumbrian Border Regiment were celebrating their takeover of the Barracks and Mess with a formal dinner night. After the after dinner speeches and Loyal Toast and the dinner over, Big Bill decided that they would have quick darts competition between the Warrant Officers and Sergeants to round the night off. The two teams were quickly selected and after a warm up, he called the two team captains together, saying, 'Right, we'll spin to see who throws first,' and taking a large silver dollar from his waistcoat pocket, he flipped it into the air and asked, 'Heads or Tails?'

The End

Epilogue

Three years later, the sun shone brightly on the empty parade square of the Junior Leaders Regiment in their barracks in Yorkshire as the spectators waited for the Inspecting Officer of the 'Pass Out Parade' to step out of his staff car and onto the dais over-looking the square. As he took up his position, an expectant hush settled over the crowd, their eyes drawn to the figure of an immaculate Junior Soldier standing proudly just to the right of the dais.

Wearing the newly issued and perfectly pressed, No2 khaki Service Dress with buttons and highly bulled studded boots gleaming in the sun, white belt with its silver buckle sitting perfectly horizontally round his waist, his neck pressed back against his collar as he looked from below his peaked forage cap; Junior Regimental Sergeant Major Jake Grundy lifted his left thigh horizontal to the ground and crashed his left boot into the tarmac of the parade square and as he came to attention he swung his Malacca cane up and under his right arm. After a pause of two seconds he stepped off and marched smartly to the front centre of the parade ground, coming smartly to a halt and standing silently for a few seconds.

Off to the right of the parade ground, three companies of Junior Soldiers and the Regimental band stood at attention in column of route, waiting for the order to march onto the square.

Jake sucked in air, expanding his chest fully and bellowed in a voice that startled some spectators and lifted birds perched in the trees surrounding the square into flight, 'JUNIOR LEADERS REGIMENT, BY THE LEFT QUICK MARCH!'

The band struck up the Regimental March as they and the three companies stepped off as one and marched toward the Regimental Square.

The line of spectators behind the seated officers and dignitaries of the front row had stood simultaneously as Jake had marched onto the square. Ian and Rafe who were studying for their A levels, grinned at each other as apprentice electrician Howard nudged the ever smiling Roger who was standing next to Nineteen year old Mike Trevelyan, George Cross; the 'Colliers' new centre forward. Mike wore his medal pinned to his blazer jacket as Jennifer stood next to him holding his hand proudly.

Tommy stood next to Mr and Mrs Edward and Jane Thompson; the ever beautiful Jane looking up at Edward standing upright, the old soldier in him caught up in the moment.

Wearing his No2 Service Dress with his General Service Medal for Malaya complete with the oak leave for his 'Mention in Dispatches, Corporal Ronnie Grundy watched his younger brother proudly as Mary held two year old Florence Grundy in her arms.

The proudest man there was Albert Grundy; flanked by eleven-year- old Billy and ten-year-old Roger, he placed a hand on each of their shoulders, looked up to the sky and said, 'That's wor lad flo!'

About the same time; newly commissioned, acting Captain Bill Armstrong MM, drove out of Haig Barracks with his new wife Rebecca and headed south for Warminster where he was due to take up his new post as an instructor at The School of Infantry.

In Ashington, the pump mounted on the back of a council wagon was started up and the dark stinking water in the quarry at Sheepwash began to be pumped out and into the river Wansbeck below as the

Council finally began the task of emptying and making safe the dangerous site.

Acknowledgement

My deepest thanks go to my dear Beth, whose help, advice and encouragement made this book possible.

My thanks also go to that select band of people who frequent the cyber 'Haway Inn' and 'Ashington Remembered' whose support and encouragement were a great inspiration

Geordie/Pitmatic words used in this book

Aah	I
Aaful	awful
Aalreet	alright
Aah've	I have
Alen	alone
An	own
Aroond	around
Bairn	Baby or small child
Bait	food carried to work
Boond	bound
Cannit	cannot
Cowld	cold
Cyek	cake
Daad	strike
Dee	do
Div	do
Divvint	do not
Doot	doubt
Droon	drown
Fyece	face
Forst	first
Fund	found
Gan	go
Gannin	going
Gis	give me
Grund	ground
Gully	large knife

Hoy	throw
Hurd	heard
He'ssell	himself
Hev	have
Hevn't	have not
Hoo	how
Haway	come on
Hord	heard
Iviry	every
Ivvor	ever
Kna	know
Lavvies	lavatory
Lowp	leap
Mair	more
Marra	friend or workmate
Mek	make
Mesell	myself
Nee	no
Nen	none
Nettie	lavatory
Nivvor	never
Nur	no
Nowt	nothing
Ower	over
Owld	old
Owt	anything
Plodgin	paddling
Reet	right
Roond	round
Sackless	dozy

Shows	the fair
Shull	shovel
Sowldgers	soldiers
Sumat	something
Taak	talk
Tecking	taking
Tha	they're
Tetties	potatoes
Thowt	thought
Towld	told
Tyeble	table
Whey	well
Willicks	winkles
Winnit	will not
Wiv	with
Wor	our
Worsells	ourselves
Yarking	beating
Ye	you
Yor	your
Yorsell	yourself

Printed in Great Britain
by Amazon